HORSESHOE SKY

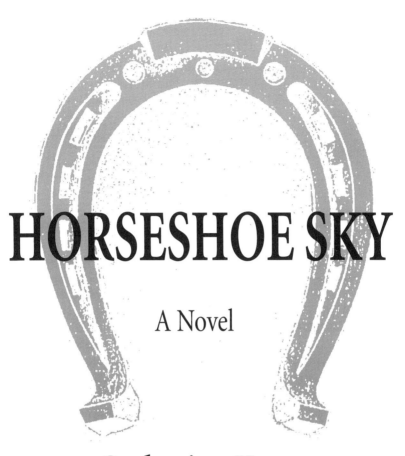

HORSESHOE SKY

A Novel

Catherine Koger

Firebrand
Books

Copyright © 1995 by Catherine Koger
All rights reserved.

This book may not be reproduced in whole or in part, except in the case of reviews, without permission from Firebrand Books, 141 The Commons, Ithaca, New York 14850.

Book design by Nightwood Design
Cover design by Lee Tackett

Printed in the United States by McNaughton & Gunn on acid-free paper

10 9 8 7 6 5 4 3 2 1

Library of Congress Cataloging-in-Publication Data

Koger, Catherine, 1948—
   Horseshoe sky : a novel / by Catherine Koger.
      p. cm.
   ISBN 1-56341-061-3 (paper : alk. paper). —ISBN 1-56341-062-1 (cloth : alk. paper)
   I. Title.
PS3561.O352H67   1995
813'.54—dc20   95-36586
                                                              CIP

ACKNOWLEDGMENTS

My grateful thanks to Nancy Bereano, the Quake City Writers' Group—Melissa, Leslie, Kim, and Jay—and to my happy friends for their undying excitement.

For Maria

1

Summer came quietly, stretching out between brittle, immortal bones, the desert's faded gems. If I sat still enough, I could see them glisten. Pale red hills were dotted with green, and the bluest skies pushed mightily down on the ridges. Giant saguaro cactus directed lonely travelers along the winding roads between Tucson and the Mexican border's prickly mountains to the southeast. Stretching under the sun, shadowed canyons filled with cicadas that screamed in unison from their perches in mesquite and palo verde trees. Their high-pitched buzzing was intended to scare fearful strangers away from this old, vulnerable land.

The tiny town of Bisbee clung to the slopes of Tombstone Canyon, waiting out the passing world. But the sounds of canyon-muffled hammers and saws reminded us all that things were changing in this dusty bottom corner of Arizona. Bisbee, home of the dead, once-famous Copper Queen Mine, reached up the curvy canyon with old brick and faded turquoise wood. The small miners' shacks hidden in the canyon, many abandoned for years, were being discovered. Turned into homes by painters, writers, hermits, Hell's Angels, and me. And Tombstone Canyon hid our lives from the seething giant hole only two miles away.

The world's largest open pit copper mine, Flagg Pit, was long defunct, but not before it encroached upon and ate half a town. Lowell, Arizona ended abruptly at the brink of hell. Half a town was no place to live, no place to be born, but people hung on to the edge of that pit with one hand and kept Lowell going with the other. Bisbee averted its eyes and clung desperately to its steep red hills.

It was July now, and we were all used to the heat. I sat in the shade on the porch of the Copper Queen Hotel, a grand brick survivor still drawing visitors to its proud, sagging body, my boots holding my legs up on the porch rail. A tumbleweed snuck across the dusty stretches of desert and died in a brittle wash. Lizards stilled themselves in specks of shade under sagebrush and greasewood. Cradling a big glass of ice tea, I pondered the stillness in my bones, the siesta in my soul. As I sipped, the coy coolness of the ice tea streamed down through my chest and disappeared. I was evaporating.

Around the corner, my little cafe—Tia Tortilla—went about its business without me, caught in the spell of the pretty teenage granddaughter of an old Mexican miner who lived up at the end of the canyon. When I hired Celita to help out after school, it was just so I could slow down a little and sit once in a while. She waited tables and worked the cash register, while I created strange tortilla sandwiches that won the hearts of Bisbee. I could wrap up just about anything in a big tortilla. When Celita's last year of high school was over, she quickly convinced me that she should do the cooking and order supplies, her cousin could wait tables, and I could relax. I was just about old enough to be her mother, but not to retire. She somehow figured that at thirty-three I deserved better. I liked to humor her, but I wasn't sure if I would like relaxing all of the time.

As I sat peering out over my half-full glass, out over the porch railing, out over my boot toes, someone walked onto the big porch through the hotel door. I looked over to see Carla, squinting at the day and opening a new pack of Juicy Fruit. She noticed me plopped down in the shade.

"Pretty dang hot out here, Kate. Why don't you come on inside and talk to me a while?"

"I'm fine here. Can't move." I watched her feverishly working her fresh stick of gum. Carla had been in charge of the front desk at the hotel forever. Hardly missed a day. When Carla's hair started turning gray, she bleached it to keep her blonde looks, and that day, as always, several long strands escaped their bobby-pinned pile at the back of her head.

"Well, everything's OK on the porch, I guess. Time to go back in." Carla was quite visible in her red Bermuda shorts, matching lipstick, and red-and-white checkered shirt.

"I snuck an early lunch in the dining room. Ate too much." She looked at her belly, which was stretching her shirt's buttonholes, distorting the square checks. "I'm going to pop." As she went inside, I saw her bird legs moving like sticks under her hanging middle, her white knees embarrassed and trapped between knee socks and the hem of her red shorts. I smiled. Where would we all be without Carla?

People walked by on the old wooden sidewalk out front, moving slowly in the heat. It was getting to be lunchtime, and I wondered if they were heading for Tia Tortilla to cool off in the ceiling fan's breeze, to see Celita with her big smile, bending over tables with her steamy black hair, making sure everyone was doing OK.

Tia and Celita were having a love affair, predestined, and not really having anything to do with me. The cafe had been waiting for her to come along from that first day when I hung the *Open* sign in the window with an annoying tremble in my hands. In this busy, crackling summer, Celita *was* Tia Tortilla, and you would've thought she had been for longer than just this young lifetime. She was responsible for the cafe's laughter that rolled through the screen door every morning and afternoon. The laughter clashed now and again with the grimy meanness peeling loudly out of the dim red bar at the end of the dusty block. St. Elmo's.

While Celita increased profits, I did just what I was doing on that scorching July day, boots up on the rail, most every afternoon, until the sun left behind a red sky and a quiet sigh. Off and on I hunted the desert for treasures which adorned the cafe's old stone walls—skulls, serapes, old photographs of cowgirls and miners, neon saguaros. I dreamed on the Copper Queen's porch, critiqued passersby, chatted with my favorites.

My glass was almost empty, only an ice puddle left. It was high noon, and the sun had gone behind a small stray cloud, when I saw a car pull up and stop, perfectly framed between the points of my boots. A twist of fate had found my lap.

I watched over the railing, my neck stretching like a periscope until I became embarrassed, pulled my feet down, and sat up straight and normal. A lanky woman unfolded her desert-colored body out of an old, well-worn black jeep. Little dust devils followed her boots as she turned to shut the creaky door. She hesitated for the dust to settle before she came up the stairs onto the porch, then stopped at the hotel door, took off her sunglasses, and wiped the road from her face with a pale bandanna. As she tucked it back into her jeans pocket, she slowly turned her face toward me. I don't think I was breathing. I knew I couldn't look at her face. Instead, I peered into my glass as if I were trying to read my fortune in a half inch of water with little floating pieces of tea-stained lemon. I suddenly inhaled and twisted my head to the side, throwing my eyes straight to hers. A moment which I could hardly tolerate. I exhaled, gazing at a face which at once made me feel sad and excited. A smile stretched across her face as she walked toward me. My head whipped back to my glass. My ears were ringing. Red roads in my brain widened. My pony fidgeted.

"Hi." The longest, most drawn-out *hi* I'd ever heard. I looked up as she flipped her thumb back toward the hotel door. "Are you staying here?" Her voice slid into the still air like a slick snake. She had dark eyes, two black coals set deeply beneath the sun of her blonde hair.

"Uh, no, I live here in town, but if you're considering staying here, it's a great place." I shifted in my chair and plopped a leg back up on the rail. A long arm reached out from her sleeveless black T-shirt, and she put a hand on the rail next to my boot, leaned into it, and looked out across the road.

"How far is the mine?" She spoke into the sun.

"The Copper Queen?" The real mine. Flagg Pit didn't count in Bisbee.

"Yeah." Her eyes took in mine. I felt an odd sense of familiarity and a sense of calm, of a lovely doom.

"See that hilltop straight ahead?" I pointed over the sloping roof of the building across the street. "With those long cracks in it toward the left? The Copper Queen Mine is in that hill."

Her eyes narrowed as she studied the short distance.

"That mine isn't operating anymore," I said, in case that mattered.

"I know." She glanced back at the hotel door and said, "Well, I guess I'll get checked in. See ya." She turned smack into Celita, who was rushing up the stairs. They all but knocked each other down.

"Kate!" Celita was frantic, and unimpressed with the incredible stranger. She grabbed my arm and pulled me out of my chair, knocking my glass over and spilling my unknown little fortune through the cracks in the wooden floor.

"What the hell's wrong? What happened?"

She pulled me down the steps. "Pop Walker's in the cafe! Hurry up, you've got to see him, he's so old!"

"OK, honey, calm down, I'm coming." I put my arm around her, turned back to my stranger, and said, "If you're hungry, I've got a little cafe around the corner. Tia Tortilla. Come on over...." I could feel her eyes on the back of my head long after we were out of sight.

Pop Walker was always a sight to see, but that dark-eyed stranger clung to my eyes. I had seen Pop before, a few times, sipping whiskey in the Crystal Palace Saloon in Tombstone. He had on the same black Stetson, black shirt, black pants, black boots, and white Custer hair and mustache. Lint everywhere. He made my cafe look like the Gunslinger Wax Museum. Sitting in the front corner, he ignored the kids surrounding him, buzzing like bees.

"OK, let Mr. Walker eat in peace. Kids! Go! Go go go go!" They split to the four winds, screeching with glee.

Celita sat down across the table from Pop, twisting her dirty white apron in her young red-tipped fingers. "You want a root beer?"

Pop looked at her, stopped chewing, and shook his head once. He remained silent, and I asked Celita to please take care of the waiting customers. Where was her cousin? I went over to Pop's side, leaned over, and whispered to him, "Sorry for the disturbance. Enjoy your food, Mr. Walker." He ignored me. I sat at the counter watching him, my arms folded across my chest, remembering the blonde stranger, then spun around in slow motion on the stool. Pop's presence competed for my attention. What the hell was Pop Walker doing in Bisbee, in my cafe? How did he get here? Must be a hundred, and as thin and wiry as a reed. He wasn't even packing a six-gun like I remembered. But he looked older, whiter—like chalk.

"Celita!" She was lost in a cloud of smoke over the grill. "Celita!"

"What!" the cloud said.

"Pop come in here by himself?"

"I don't know. He was just suddenly sitting there at that table. Baby told me who he was."

Celita's cousin appeared out of the bathroom accompanied by a shield of stale cigarette fumes.

"Baby, please don't smoke in the bathroom!" Baby was fifteen and about due for a new name. And to me, there was something disgusting about smoking in bathrooms. "Smoke outside, or over there near the counter."

She frowned at me and rolled her eyes for Celita, still invisible but her whereabouts known. "OK," Baby muttered. "I can tell you where Pop Walker came from." Baby had good ears. I waited the appropriate amount of time. She continued. "Some woman brought him in here. Pulled up in a black jeep, helped him out, and sat him at that table. She told me he was Pop Walker." She rolled her eyes again. "Then she just left him here. I kept asking him what he wanted, he just kept saying 'Get out.' So I brought him a Cactus Creole Roll. He seems to like it OK."

Pop Walker and my dark-eyed stranger! Looking for the dead mine. My smile began a long journey, no looking back. Was she a relative of his? I didn't think Pop had relatives. He was one of the few gunfighters left from the wild days when Tombstone was hopping with silver. Stories had it that Pop rode with Wyatt Earp. But that would make him about a hundred and fifty.

There was no doubt he knew all the ghosts in the silvered mountains from Bisbee to Tucson. He knew hidden graves. He knew never-told secrets—you could see it in the set of his mouth and the distance in his eyes. He was a lonesome man dressed in black who didn't talk much. I had always liked watching him in the old Tombstone saloon: he would make the silent ghosts come alive for me on the winding hour-long drive back to Bisbee.

But I'd never known him to venture from Tombstone. He was kind of a local tourist attraction, propped up in the Crystal Palace, his holstered six-gun hanging off a bony hip, tipping his whiskey glass like a gentleman, and giving few words to the curious.

I figured she'd come for him, so I waited. I waited for an hour. I went over to see if he needed anything.

"Water."

"OK, Pop." I brought him a big glass of cold water, which he sipped quietly, in his fashion.

Another half hour went by. Celita and I stared at Pop, and Baby cleaned up after the last customer. Time to close. I thought I'd go over to the hotel and look for the owner of a black jeep. "Celita, watch Pop. I'll be back in a few minutes."

The lobby was empty except for Carla behind the desk. I rang the bell anyway and grinned.

"Hey, Katie darlin', what are you up to?" She greeted me in between smacks of chewing gum, blowing a loose strand of hair up and away from her face only for it to drift back down for more.

"I'm looking for somebody. This somebody left her elderly friend in my cafe, and I think he's wondering where she is so he can go home. Celita's got to close." I looked around the empty lobby. "She checked in here a couple hours ago, I don't know her name and, uh, he can't remember it." I guess I could have asked him.

Carla cocked her head to one side. "Blonde? Real cute? Black T-shirt? Long arms?"

"Uh-huh. Yeah." I gave away my delight to Carla's squint.

"Mattie Springer. Rooms 204 and 206." She didn't even have to look at the register.

"That's good. Two rooms? OK. Thanks a million." I flew up the red-carpeted stairs which spiraled under an ancient chandelier, then stopped about half way and yelled down to Carla, "Hey, Carla! How long's she staying?"

"Indefinitely's what she told me!"

My hand gripped the smooth polished rail and my eyebrows sat up straight. I walked slowly up the rest of the stairs and turned right for 204.

2

Beecham Street in Lowell was named after some old Arizona politician. His great-grandson, Billy Beecham, lived in the newest house on the street. And the biggest. He owned the hardware store in Lowell, and his wife, Janice, kept his books. The store had been in his family forever, managing to escape the appetite of the expanding pit mine.

Billy was doing good by his family responsibility. Janice hated the store. Janice hated Lowell, but Billy didn't know it. I knew because Celita babysat their six-year-old son Ronald when they went out. Celita told me that Janice kept a hidden stash of Smirnoff vodka behind the stereo console. She drank it with orange juice at night, when there was no arithmetic to keep her from herself. Celita heard Janice and Billy fighting in their bedroom one night after they returned from having dinner out.

"Janice, you're drunk,"

"Now, Billy, don't be mad, honey. I just had me a little bit to calm my nerves."

Billy yelled, "You're drunk! You've got to stop! This is embarrassing!"

"Billy, shh! Shh! Celita will hear you. Go on and take her home. Don't wake up Ronnie. Go on now, honey, don't be upset." She ushered him out of the room and closed the door after him.

Celita loved to babysit for them because they had cable and she could watch MTV, although Ronnie whined.

Last year, Billy Beecham started a sightseeing business in the Copper Queen Mine. He got an electric four-car rail train up in Phoenix that the zoo had used a long time ago for tours. The cars didn't have sides on them, just a red roof and red seats. Billy used it to take tourists in one of the tunnels that wound through the hilly earth. Four days a week, tourists could go into the mine and look at its lifelessness. I heard most of the tunnels weren't safe, but Billy had the main tunnel retimbered.

Turrell Fisher collected the seven-dollar fee and drove the train, telling the history of the mine and some far-fetched legends over a loudspeaker to the tourists as they looked out the windows at the lit-up rock walls. But not too many tourists came. That train was never full as it squeaked its way through the earth. Turrell drank most nights at St. Elmo's. At least every night that I walked by there I could see him at the bar through the always-open door.

Billy was a smart man. He had to be to keep a thriving hardware business in Lowell, but he didn't look smart. He had no clear, defined, confident features greeting the world. And I thought that train was a stupid idea, not a smart one. Hiring Turrell wasn't smart, either. Turrell seemed like the kind of man you couldn't count on. I heard that he neglected his ailing mother until she died of malnutrition. And that he'd left two wives so far, and several children, in Texas. He put a gray film of a little despair, a little I-don't-care, and a lot of hostility over his face for the world. Turrell lived in Lowell, too, but not in a house like Billy Beecham's. I guessed he drank in Bisbee so he wouldn't run into his boss drunk.

But it could've happened. Every now and then Janice and Billy would have dinner in Bisbee at the hotel. After dinner they'd sit in the bar, which Janice loved and Billy disliked. No one really shared conversation with them. People just slid past them in the dim, lively room. No one ever stopped to put an arm around a shoulder to see how they were doing and catch a quick laugh. Billy sat silent while Janice looked around like a bird, her smile turning on and off when she caught someone's eye. Her long cigarettes gave her something to do with her hands, but she didn't have anything to do with Billy. I would nod a greeting to her, just short of stopping and whispering in her ear that she leave Billy and head for the hills.

I didn't care for Billy, or Turrell, or the sightseeing train. I figured Turrell would wreck that train some dark day.

One night I dropped Celita off at the Beechams' to babysit in a thunderstorm so loud she could hardly hear a tipsy Janice whisper in her ear as she let her in, "Honey, one day I'm going to get on Billy's train and never come back. I'm going to ride in that thing forever. I'll be the real Copper Queen."

So I always thought Janice should drive that train, not Turrell, and give up keeping Billy's books at the store. She'd be free. And she would entertain her admiring, squinting, hard-hatted tourists as they jiggled along the metal rails deeper into the mine.

As I knocked on 204 I knew, somehow, that behind this door, ready to snap its fingers at my newly paused life, limitless possibility waited. It opened. Mattie Springer's face was tired, vulnerable, beautiful. I felt it tug at mine. The light hair around her forehead and temples was damp with sweat. The deep, deep darkness of her eyes seemed to drift in their confined circles. I felt my eyes become rock climbers, pulling, almost on the top. Some sort of trancelike dare took over, and we didn't budge until a door down the hall banged us out of each other's eyes. I was on the verge of tipping over, but instead I heard myself saying, "Look, I don't mean to bother you, um—"

"Come on in." She moved aside, and I stepped in next to her. She shut the door with one hand and held the other out to me. "My name's Mattie."

"Kate." I took her hand, and for that brief moment I held onto her for a lifetime.

She sat on the bed and looked down at the big silver turquoise ring on her hand while she waited for me to speak. I took a few awkward steps around the small room, noticing the flowered wallpaper, the heavy brass bedposts, the lace curtains stirring at the open window.

"Pop's down at my cafe and he's finished eating," I said gently, standing next to the windowsill.

She slapped her knees and pushed herself up from the bed, sighing to me, "Let's go get him." Then she picked up her keys from the dresser along with her sunglasses and a pack of cigarettes. She smiled and took my hand, leading me out the door and down the hall. We stopped at the top of the stairs, and Mattie put her arm around my shoulders. "Kate"—our noses were an inch apart—"Pop and I need

an escort, a bodyguard, a tour guide. Can you help us?"
My face nodded, my heart ran wild through the hills. She nodded, too, squeezed my shoulder, and down the stairs we went.
Carla frowned as she watched us cross the lobby. Two gals, hapless compadres, side by side. Before we went into the cafe, curiosity put my hand on Mattie's arm and stopped us at the door. "Can I talk with you, about Pop, sometime? Maybe tonight?"
"Yeah. Let's take a walk. It would be nice to walk. Meet me on the hotel porch. Eight-thirty?"
"Good. OK."
"Hey, Pop." Mattie tried to help him out of his chair, without his cooperation. "Let's go for a ride, take a look at this big ol' dead mine." As I watched from the doorway, they moved slowly away, disappearing into the dreamy afternoon shade. I barely noticed Celita slide past me on her way out, mumbling something about overtime. I suddenly needed to shake from head to tail like a wet dog.

3

Up the canyon, a large mesquite tree threw a breeze into my kitchen. The tea kettle screamed long after I yanked it off the stove. Dogs barked across the canyon, and I heard old Francisco yelling for Celita. Dusk was around the corner. Behind the ridge, yellow thunderheads gave up their late-day efforts and left quietly.

I drank my tea on the front porch, my little house comforting me as I leaned back against it. I felt the smooth, weathered wood at my back, imagined the tin roof in a rain storm and the wood-stove smoke leaving the chimney through a winter sky. I smelled the still heat of the old walls, heard the middle-of-the-night creaking of a ghost miner's family.

Now I sat where the outside met the inside, where sounds mingled into a sweet call from an old dream. The curtain came out of the open window just above me and stroked my settling head. My house and I liked the dusk the best, because it was then that we were equal, the same hue, the same sigh. All my life I had hated turning on the lights when it became too dark outside to see anything inside. The curtain danced like a flag out the window, joyous in its freedom. I shut my eyes and saw my mother flitting through our house flipping on all the light switches, muttering to me in her Georgia drawl about how strange it was to have a little girl who liked to sit and stare in the dark. I think I had tried hard to be still so that she would become still and know the peace of the dusk, so that all her chores would just drift up into the dim sky.

My phone rang and cut short my time travel. It was Thea. "Hey, Cactus!" Her gravelly voice delighted in the sound of her designated nickname for me.

"Quit smoking," I said for the millionth time as I grudgingly turned on the lights.

"Hey, listen."

She ignored my command and started pushing her voice through my stomach with no regard to twilight's hush. Thea had always been a pusher, and through all the years we had been together I had never really caught my breath. Until the night I left her crying into her dinner plate, trying to light a cigarette, and moved up the canyon. She never knew about the nights I cried like a lonesome coyote afraid of the night. We managed to make Bisbee belong to each of us, individually, after that. We had settled into being occasional friends, covered with a thin dust of familiarity. I had always been able to call in the dusk to surround me, to help protect me from intruders with weapons sent by the world to harass my soul. This had come in handy with Thea around.

Now her excited voice told me about a dream Marta had had a couple of nights ago. She gave me all the details, expecting me to be astonished. In the dream, Marta had been standing in the giant open pit mine, alone, on a bright blue day. Suddenly, General Robert E. Lee appeared in the distance on his horse, Traveler, and walked right up next to her. Thea said Marta was a wreck all the next day and wouldn't leave the house. She thought the dream meant she should go back home to Virginia. Marta was like that—afraid of herself. I thought it was a great dream and said that I would have gone right down to the pit, climbed into it, stood smack in the middle, and waited. I would definitely have some questions to ask General Lee's ghost. So I was no comfort to either of them. We said good-bye and hung up. It was seven forty-five.

I smiled at myself in the mirror as I brushed my hair back from my face. My excitement looked good in a fresh white long-sleeved shirt. I wiped the dust off my boots, stared into the mirror, and imagined Mattie. Both of us were the tint of the rocky hills faded into flesh, a reflection of the burnt red earth. I was a little taller. Her short blonde hair gave her face a crispness, eager to cut the sky with its leading edge. My face pulled long dusky hair behind it, like a team of horses champing at the bit. Mattie faded, and for the first time I saw behind me, in the mirror, that my house was bigger than I thought, its rooms were larger, its lungs full and strong.

Francisco yelled again for Celita. His sound rose up over the hill and off to the north behind me as I walked down the canyon to the hotel. I hadn't told Thea about Mattie Springer. I didn't know what to say.

Mattie had just come out of the bar onto the porch when I arrived at the hotel. She had half a beer to go and was lighting a cigarette when I walked up to her. She looked at me from boots to ears as she shook the match in the air. "Hi." She slowly exhaled the smoke from her cigarette. The match died, but its flame was instantly reincarnated to live in my belly. I managed a serious "Hi" back.

"You want something to drink?" She gestured to her beer as she sat down lightly.

"Sure. I'll get it. Be right back." I came back with a sarsaparilla and sat down in the broad wooden chair next to her. We let a smooth silence drop over us as we watched the night sky take shape. Brilliant stars appeared over black silhouetted ridges and peaks. Crickets woke up singing. The sky grew to enormity, filling itself with constellations and the scooting dots of satellites. A screech owl threw its voice down the canyon.

"Pop should see this," Mattie said, admiring the jeweled sky spread above her. "It's been a long time since I've been to Bisbee." She looked at me. "He's up in his room snoring away."

"Where do you live?" I asked her quietly, not wanting to spoil her contentment with the stars.

"Tucson. Too many lights in that city to see stars like this. The big telescope up at the observatory can barely pick them up anymore, and it's fifty miles away out in the desert. I've always had to go someplace else for a sky like this. Thirty-three years of looking for a real sky." She smiled to herself.

We were the same age. "Where do you go...to see stars like this?"

"Camping up in the mountains, in the Chiricahuas. While I'm there I look for Cochise's grave." She taunted me with a crooked smile.

I leaned my head back on the chair. "I heard he's supposed to be buried there, but only the Apaches know where. No white person will ever find him."

"Wouldn't want to, but I look anyway." She glanced back at the

Dipper, back at Orion, back at Cochise, took the last sip from her bottle, and stood up with a contented sigh. I was ready. Ready to walk, to climb, to fly, to laugh in starry space with this perfect stranger.

"What do you say we stretch our legs?" Her voice surrounded me. I put my empty bottle down and stood up.

As I led Mattie up Opera Drive toward the trail across Buckman Ridge, my mother's voice flew in from far, far away, invading for a moment the enchantment of the new night. I could see her in a clear flash, standing at the window of my loaded-down truck, eight years ago, in an early morning warm Georgia rain. I was heading west, for some kind of chunky gold. She reached in and put her hand over mine on the steering wheel. The engine was running. "Honey," she squeezed my hand gently, "be good to yourself, and be careful."

There, under a billion stars, heading out over the ridge with Mattie Springer, I knew I could do both.

We moved silently along the old wagon road below the ridge, passing the still, dim shapes of sagebrush and rock outcrops. The stars charged the air, coyotes moaned in the distant hills. Mattie moved alongside me, hands in her pockets, watching her steps. I knew the road well and looked at the sky as I walked, wondering at the familiarity I was feeling. I sensed I had known Mattie for a long, long time. Why didn't that make me uncomfortable? I looked at her. She was scanning the stars off to her side, off to the fall of the ridge, off to the distance beyond distant. She slowed down, pulled to a stop by a trillion stars. I stood next to her.

"These stars, all these stars, it seems like they're trying to tell me something. Trying to remind me of something." She looked at me. "Some particular brilliance I used to know." As I nodded, I realized I wasn't breathing. "There's even something familiar about this night," she continued, turning back to the glittered sky. "Something familiar about you."

My legs were concrete slabs, my head light as a feather. I couldn't speak. Mattie faced me with a hint of astonishment on her otherwise confused face. I pointed up to the stars.

"Orion. The Dipper. Jupiter?" She was right. I felt as if I had known these stars, these planets, and Mattie, well before they all had names.

As Mattie gazed upward, she spoke to me by way of a sky bound to secrecy. "There's something going on here." It was a proclamation.

I turned to her. "What—" My eyes reflected the answer. Her face turned from the stars and she spoke to my mouth. "I don't know. Something."

"Something what?" My lowered voice felt that this was unbearable.

"Well...you, something." She started walking, and my legs kicked in next to her.

Excited now, concrete legs turning to warm flesh, I tried to walk with my body turned toward her, like a little fiddler crab. "It's weird, it does feel like I've known you for a long time."

"I know. That's the way I feel. Like somehow I can't do what I came here to do without you. So this thing I'm doing with Pop isn't just about Pop anymore. It's about you, too." She forced the words and couldn't look at me. "This is really strange."

The night teemed with a stirring, a warning, a welcome. What was about me too? What was strange? What kind of tour guide was I going to be? I settled into a regular stride and asked Mattie to tell me about what she was doing with Pop.

"Pop talked me into coming here. Wants me to help him find someone. But you need to know that he lives in two worlds. The one we see him in now, and the one that's dearest to him. So he goes back and forth. Sometimes he's mean, sometimes he's nice. Sometimes he's like a lone, dusty feather at the mercy of the wind. Sometimes he's a handsome respected gunfighter." Mattie looked around her as she walked. "Just so you know. Even though he can be difficult, I feel like I need to see this thing through. It's pretty crazy, I guess."

Mattie seemed to know Pop well, and that made me want more of him. "I don't know much about him really, other than all this gunfighter stuff," I said. "Never thought he'd end up in my life in any way."

Mattie remembered the day she first met Pop. As we walked she remembered everything, and I was the first person to hear the story.

4

Mattie had taken a job training a horse for a family friend at his ranch in Tombstone a couple of months ago. The day she drove down she felt alone, like a wandering burro, meandering through old mountains. Thunderclouds piled up ahead of her on the horizon, while cottonwoods begged their streambeds for water. On the seat next to her, a pair of worn leather work gloves slept in the sun on top of her duffle bag, and in the back of the jeep, her saddle shifted with the turns of the road.

She sang a lonely song as she passed through red rock and peering ghosts, and just outside of Tombstone, pressed a hand to the old photograph in her shirt pocket. She slid the picture out of her pocket and into the sun, and her eyes moved back and forth from her grandmother's face to the road stretching ahead. Behind her, in Tucson, three graves graced the hill at the back of her ranch, always there to catch the falling sun at the end of a day. Her grandmother, her mother, her father—little upright stones, their names calling softly to the desert valley spread out at their feet.

The giant clouds rattled loudly when she drove into Tombstone, and as the sky blackened and heavy raindrops shot down, Mattie stopped at the Crystal Palace Saloon to wait out the storm. Through the saloon's swinging doors, she was greeted by the sweet, biting smell of wet desert creosote swirling around the ceiling fan, with the occasional whiff of a cigar. She noticed Pop at the end of the bar. He was looking at her.

The thunder shook the walls and moved through her ribs as Mattie sat down at the bar, ordered coffee, and wiped a little rain from her face.

Her father taught Mattie to train horses, and she was one of the best in the area. In the year since he died, the ranch sank in Mattie's heart like a still, heavy rock, and she began to hire out more and more outside of Tucson, leaving most of the business of the ranch in her brother's hands.

Mattie and Pop were the only customers that afternoon. She smiled at him, but he stared steadily at Mattie until she became a little annoyed. She took her coffee and went over to the bar stool next to him. "What's on your mind mister?" she said, leaning into his face with tightened eyes, ready for the showdown. He smiled at her with what appeared to be a brand new set of false teeth, a little crooked. His eyes slid to a faraway time and watered up. Mattie softened and relaxed into a gentle "What...?"

Pop looked down at his thin cigar dying in the ashtray. He muttered, "Elizabeth."

Mattie felt a spark in her chest from two old stones struck together. Her mouth dropped open. *Elizabeth?* Her grandmother's name. Her father's mother. Mattie took great pride in the fact that she was the spitting image of Elizabeth Springer. It had always made her feel special, to that day, like an old, sweet secret. She pulled back a little from Pop and turned her head away, looking for help from an empty room. "Whoa...." No help was there.

The thunder moved from the saloon on to the east like a giant outlaw stomping his boots on the way out of town. In the disappearing clamor, Mattie turned to Pop and said clearly, "Elizabeth Springer?"

Pop's eyes swam in confusion as he looked into Mattie's demanding face. He stared into his whiskey glass hanging midway between his mouth and the bar, frozen in indecision. Mattie cocked her head around in front of Pop, impatient. "Excuse me!"

Pop slowly set his glass down and fixed his gaze on Mattie's eyes. Confusion had given way to a hardened glare. He touched a finger to his black hat and said, "Nice to meet you ma'am." Then he stood up neatly and walked across the floor and out the doors into the last wisps of the spent storm. Mattie spun around on her stool to watch one of the most curious moments of her life slide smoothly through the swinging doors.

The bartender tried to refill her coffee. She covered her cup with one hand, lighting a cigarette with the other. "No thanks, I've got to get going." Disappointed words enveloped in smoke. "Who was that guy?" She looked back toward the doorway.

The bartender smiled as he placed the coffee pot back on its heat. "Pop Walker. Don't pay no attention to him, he's wacky. Senile. Doesn't like to talk much anyway."

A faint memory tapped on Mattie's shoulder. "I think I've heard of him. Wasn't he a famous gunfighter or something?"

"Yep. Rode with the best of 'em. When he was just a kid he rode with Wyatt Earp. Pop hangs out in here most of the time, has for a million years. Some days he don't come out of his room though. Neighbors in the rooming house can hear him talking to himself. But he never talks to himself in here. Somebody ought to be looking after him...." He wiped the bar clean with a white towel. Another customer came in, and the bartender moved on to a different conversation.

Mattie put out her cigarette and walked to her car. *Wyatt Earp?* The low sun had just dipped behind the washed hills. The air was warm, and she could smell the left-behind rain quickly evaporating on the hard ground. As she drove away, she made plans to bring the photograph of a young Elizabeth Springer to the Crystal Palace tomorrow. Every time Mattie left the ranch, she brought a piece of it with her, and this time she was traveling with her favorite picture of Elizabeth.

The next day, she sat at the bar as another bartender chatted with two women at the cash register, ignoring her. Fresh from a shower after a hard, sweaty day working with the horse, she wanted to be presentable, arriving in a white shirt and vest, and new blue jeans. She was nervous, turning the sepia photograph over and over in her hands, catching her grandmother's dark eyes each time. On the back was stamped *J.J. Porter, Photographer. Santa Rita Road, Tucson, Arizona, January 7, 1920.*

When Elizabeth had died five years ago, Mattie's father gave her all of his mother's photographs. Much of the magic left Mattie's life with her grandmother's death. Elizabeth's stories had revealed a desert West that was one big, gripping adventure: stories of masquerading as a man in her teens and riding mustang roundups, of the opera in Tombstone on the arm of Matthew Springer, of barrel races won hands down, of reading poetry to Matthew as he slowly collapsed in the fist of tuberculosis. She taught Mattie how to love horses, how to ride, how to split the sky with a wild jump over a cowering gulch. She taught Mattie how to delight in herself.

Mattie kept the box of old photographs in her office in the stable and spent many lonely nights with those pictures, mumbling to her soul. It felt strange to her then, sitting at the bar in the Crystal Palace, one photograph separated from its companions, Elizabeth again traveling the road to Tombstone. She had been there an hour and Pop had not shown up. Interrupting the bartender's conversation, she asked, "Excuse me, can you tell me where Pop Walker lives? Uh, he was supposed to meet me here and I'm afraid he forgot and I have something he wanted me to bring him." The bartender looked at her with a suspicious eye. One of the women he was talking to asked Mattie for a light. As Mattie lit her cigarette, the woman said, "He's at Randall's Rooming House, up on Table Mountain Road, the big green house at the end." She stared at Mattie. "Are you a relative?"

Mattie wasn't used to being a stranger. Tight-lipped, she answered, "He's a friend of the family."

"Oh." Cigarette smoke drifted up past the woman's deeply lined face, past her dyed black hair, and disappeared in the ceiling fan's breeze. Her eyes narrowed. "Well, that Pop sure was well known in the old days for talkin' big. Time to time he still does, but he forgets things. Someone ought to be living with him, poor old soul. We think he's senile. Some of the ladies take meals to him, and the senior center sends him a hot meal every day at noon during the week. If he's not in his room, they'll bring it on over here. Seems the one thing he remembers to do is come over here. They do his laundry for him at the house, but Mr. Randall can only do so much."

Mattie left the woman's insinuating stare and said dryly, "Thank you very much." A scrappy kid carving his initials in the sidewalk was happy to give her directions to Table Mountain Road. It was close enough to walk. Her nervousness spread through her fingers as she knocked on the rooming house door. No one answered, so Mattie walked in. A man leaning back in a chair watched her in silence. She walked up the stairs that loomed in front of her, but stopped short as the man's voice said loudly, "What are you doing, miss?" He got up and stood at the bottom of the stairs. This must be Mr. Randall.

"I'm here to visit Mr. Walker," she announced without looking at him.

"He's probably sleeping." The gruff voice tugged at her back.

An elderly man passed her on his way down. She asked him which room was Pop's. The man pointed up the stairs. "First room on the left."

Mattie walked up to his room, leaving Mr. Randall in her dust. She stood outside the door and looked at Elizabeth's picture, ready to bargain for a little help.

After several well-paced knocks, the door creaked open just enough to fit Pop's haggard face.

"Mr. Walker, do you remember me? I need to talk to you—"

Pop shut the door in her face. She knocked again, firmer, demanding. The door opened with a jerk. Mattie shoved Elizabeth's picture up to Pop's face and held it there, like a crucifix to Dracula's surprised eyes. Pop's hand came up and gently took the photograph. Mattie let him hold it. In those next tender moments, she saw Pop's face transform from agony to joy. She waited for his words to come and help her understand. Instead, he took a step back with the picture and shut the door in her face again.

"Shit!" Mattie stood there, mouth open in exasperation, with no picture, no words from Pop. She said loudly through the closed door, "You meet me in twenty minutes in the Crystal Palace, with the picture, or I'm going to come back here and shoot this door down!" She clenched her jaw, spun around, stormed down the stairs with her hands on her hips, quivering, as if poised over two six-guns. The desert's gorgeous gunslinger, drawing out Pop Walker. As if Pop were in his room, taking his holster off the bedpost, strapping it on, tucking the photograph in a vest pocket.

Pop showed up in twenty minutes on the dot. Mattie was sitting at a table and had a whiskey poured and waiting for him.

Somehow, Mattie had figured out how to handle Pop. He saw her immediately when he came in the saloon, went straight to the table, sat down, took a gulp of whiskey, then stared at her. "What's your name?" His words were tight, fists clenched around fear.

"Where's the picture?"

Pop took off his hat, pulled the slightly bent photograph out of the crown, and put it on the table. Mattie didn't move.

"What's your name?" He put his hat back on.

Mattie slid the picture across the table to her side. "Mattie Springer." She gestured to the photograph. "Elizabeth Springer was my grandmother. She died five years ago."

Pop was staring at the photograph on the table. The smoke from Mattie's cigarette formed a thin cloud over Elizabeth's beautiful mouth, her intense eyes.

"Do you know…that she died?"

Pop's watery eyes looked from the picture to Mattie. He nodded.

Mattie leaned toward Pop across the table. "So you knew my grandmother?" She moved back in her chair and found herself smiling. "Wait here, don't you leave." She got up and went to the bar, ordered another whiskey for Pop and a beer for herself, bought a cigar, and settled in for a story that she would extract from Pop one way or another.

He filled up the space between them with thick cigar smoke, speaking with disjointed, bitter words. "The opera took her. Flimsy silk boys courting. A dream world, full of nothin'." He let out more smoke. "They all hate me. But we went to the corral, in the middle she'll come out to me." He chuckled, "She did what she wanted."

His words tumbled into confusion, making little sense. It took her a while, but Mattie was able to pick enough pieces out of his rambling to realize that he and her grandmother had been lovers. That Lizzy snuck away from the opera to be with Pop in the moon shadows of the town corral.

Apparently, Pop met Mattie's grandmother in Tombstone before Lizzy married Matthew Springer. She would go there with her aunt and uncle's family for the opera. When Mattie figured that out, she looked hard at Pop behind his cigar smoke across the table from her, struggling to remember every conversation she had ever had with Elizabeth, hoping to come up on some quick word, some indication of a taboo love affair with a gunfighter. This new magic in the shape of Pop Walker made her grandmother come alive again. She felt Elizabeth, a tiny spirit sitting on her shoulder like a parrot nonchalantly scratching itself under one spread-out wing.

"Now what other little love secrets did you have?" Mattie said to the imaginary parrot in exasperation. "A gunfighter in Tombstone …who else? Cochise?" She became aware that Pop was telling the ashtray something.

"Elizabeth is here, we'll find him. I've got to get ready," he mumbled. Mattie's head moved forward to listen closely as he cussed about some guy named Blue who, it seemed, had something to do with Wyatt Earp being trapped deep in the tunnels of the Copper Queen. Mattie was hooked. Pop was hers. What the hell was he talking about?

"Hey!" She jerked him out of his one-way conversation. His face took on a blank look as he gazed past her. With his cigar jutting from the corner of his mouth like a little smokestack pulling a rattling train, he got up and walked out the door.

A tender breeze met us at the top of the ridge, and we rested on an old wagon carcass in the lingering air of her story. My legs dangled from the wagon, and I swished them past each other as Mattie sat still and silent. I waited. She gave the night a long sigh and looked back down the starlit trail.

"It was really an incredible thing, but it also felt so normal. A demented old man living in a world no one else knew, suddenly, in one leap of memory, lands in my life. It wasn't something I could walk away from." Mattie ran her fingers through her hair and left her hands clasped together on the back of her neck. "He's latched onto me like a brittle old claw, and if he lets go, I won't be able to put the pieces back together. Now I've got him here and I don't know what the hell's going to happen."

She looked at me as if she expected an answer. But I only had three million questions.

"My grandmother's lover! He told me some things I could hardly believe—Wyatt Earp trapped in the Copper Queen Mine! How do you believe or not believe something like that? But I guess that's not the point." She looked out over the dim hilltops and took us back to Tombstone.

Mattie had seen Pop every day for a couple of weeks until the horse was trained and she had to return to Tucson. He didn't seem to understand or give any credibility to her explanation that she was leaving but would be back the next weekend to see him. She was in Tombstone again in three days. Mattie couldn't think of anything else but Pop's story. He demanded, begged that she take him to find Wyatt, to rescue him in the mine. She didn't tell anyone about Pop. Pop and her grandmother. Pop and Wyatt Earp.

"Pop would be waiting in the saloon like he was expecting me.

Even through the blur of his memory, he seemed to know I was coming. I went every few days and stayed in a motel. I felt like a vagrant. My brother wasn't happy that I was gone so much, but I didn't really care. Pop was driving me crazy trying to get me to agree to take him to the mine.

"I spent some time talking with people who knew Pop. They all said he was nuts and they liked to talk about his fame as a gunfighter more than his state of disrepair. One old guy told me that Pop had just appeared in Tombstone a long time ago—dirty and thirsty, looking older than his young years, complaining that somebody stole his horse and left him in the mountains to rot. So he settled there, took up gambling, kept his six-guns shiny, and told many stories about his narrow misses riding with Wyatt Earp. And some people believed him, especially the kids. One of those kids was this old guy I was talking to. He said, 'Maybe he never did ride with Earp. But Earp was his hero, he talked about him all the time. No reason to take that away from him now.' A dedicated fan, and he was right."

Mattie put her hands on her hips and looked ahead down her unfamiliar path. "Somebody else told me they heard way back when that Pop first showed up in Tombstone after he was robbed of a silver claim out near Gleeson. Who knows if being a gunfighter was a better identity than being a failed prospector. Anyway, Pop entertained Tombstone—everyone seems to hold him in their hearts in one way or another. They certainly care enough to check on him and help him out. Remind him of things. But no one had to remind him to get over to the Crystal Palace."

I was a little bewildered. Wyatt Earp trapped in the mine? I was starting to take this seriously and felt ridiculous. Wyatt Earp was long dead and buried in California, many, many miles from this ridge and from Pop's looney tale. But here was Mattie, standing in front of me in the starlight, consumed by the story. An ugly voice came into my head, adding to my confusion. It was Turrell I heard, over the loudspeaker, on his stupid train tour, telling tourists from San Francisco and Phoenix about a ghost who lived way back deep in one of the tunnels. Some angry miner thrashing around in the ether because he was murdered. Now and then dust from his thrashing would come shooting out of the mine and hang in a swirling cloud over the highway, messing up traffic. Something like that.

Mattie was shaking my shoulder. "Kate, hey. Where did you

go?" It was as if I'd left and been gone hours. Way back in the mine.

"Sorry. Mattie, did you bring Pop here to help him find Wyatt Earp? Because he thinks you are Elizabeth? Wyatt Earp died when Pop was just a young man. He was married and living in California before he died. How could Pop have ridden with him, and how can he think Wyatt Earp is stuck in that mine, just about a hundred and twenty years old! Doesn't make sense."

Mattie chuckled. "No, it doesn't. And it doesn't do any good to tell him Wyatt Earp is dead. There's something underneath all this. Something that is somehow real, that I can't know yet. Anyway, I believe I have to follow it through. It does have to do with my grandmother, though, like she wants me to help Pop, or maybe I think I'm going to find out something I need to know." She looked down at her boots and her voice spread out low over the ground. "I've thought about this. I haven't thought of much else—it won't let me go. And I really think Lizzy is calling the shots here."

The stars came down and silenced us for a while. My mind was off racing with satellites that peeked at us from above. The silence grew. Pop Walker had been Mattie's grandmother's lover. Pop Walker had some delusion that he had to save Wyatt Earp, trapped in the Copper Queen Mine. And people say there is a ghost in the mine. And Lizzy Springer's spirit was orchestrating it all. I suddenly felt crowded. I thought maybe Pop was confusing Earp with this other fellow, this Copper Queen ghost. Mattie wasn't overly excited about the ghost in the mine when I told her the story, but I was.

"You don't think there's some connection? Two different people in a tunnel in the Copper Queen? One a ghost and one the oldest human alive."

"You can't take this literally, Kate. It's his mind, it's haywire."

"It's not really literal. It's incredible."

"It's a coincidence."

We sat close on the rusted wagon frame. I was pouting a little over her dismissing the mine ghost as coincidence. I knew there were no coincidences in life. Everything existed at the front end of intention. If she believed her dead grandmother was calling the shots here, then what was so odd about considering the synchronicity of a dead miner's ghost living in the mine?

"Mattie, you don't think that I'm a coincidence, do you?" It was a sweet challenge.

She touched my cheek with her fingertips, and then, folding her arms across her chest and pushing a sound out from her mouth, she said, "I don't know, Kate. I don't know. You are, uh, I don't know. I don't know why you seem so important, so loving. I don't know why you are here, now, with me, under all these stars, talking about a goddamn ghost in a mine. I don't know why I'm crying, I don't know." She tried to pull back the few tears that had squeezed out and to calm the exasperated quiver in her voice.

I couldn't move. My mouth hung open as I slowed the rhythm of the waves rolling through my body. There was nothing else to do but kiss her, which I was a moment away from doing when she got up, lit a cigarette, and started pacing around the wagon. I sat there, staring straight ahead.

She moved around and around that wagon, making me dizzy. The stars swirled in the sky, and I brushed my hands over my face, firmly. I laughed. Pop was crazy, desperate, and he sucked Mattie in like the sky sucked in the stars. If Mattie was Pop's link to Lizzy and a time long buried in pain, then who was I? I was Mattie's link to the mine, and to the stars. The picture was complete. From the grave to the living secret to the pulse of the cosmos. I popped up off that dead wagon in a shot and went to pace with Mattie. This was no coincidence.

5

The next morning, bright against the hot, blue sky, I walked down to the cafe feeling fresh, like a new coat of white paint on a worn wooden fence. The cafe's screen door banged twice behind me as I stretched a finger across the warm fried air to Celita at the stove and made my way through the tables. "Pop's going to be eating lunch here every day for a while. Don't charge him. Let him sit as long as he wants until you close. He's accustomed to that; we'll pick him up." I plopped down on a stool, reached behind the counter, and grabbed a handful of chips. I sat munching, waiting for Celita's response. She looked back toward me as she stirred a pot of black beans. "That's OK."

Not much of a response. Pop was famous in this dusty, whispering corner of the world. I thought she'd think this was quite an event. I shrugged my shoulders and headed for the door, giving Baby's long dark braid an affectionate tug as I slid past her.

Celita's tight voice stopped me as my hand went for the door. "Kate, um, can my grandfather come too? To sit with Pop? And eat lunch too, at no charge?" The words were fast, forced. I turned around. She was leaning over the counter, young and nervous, waiting. The clatter of forks, knives, plates, and talking froze in silence over the tables. I remembered Celita telling me how she worried about her grandfather because he wouldn't, or couldn't, fix himself lunch when she was working. And if she made it ahead of time in the morning, like I had suggested, he would only eat it some of the time.

And Francisco was poor, probably living on a meager miner's pension. I never asked Celita how she came to live with him. I didn't know much about Francisco, and it occurred to me that Celita took care of him, not the other way around. It also occurred to me that Pop might never utter a word to Francisco. The silent three-hour lunch. But that was all right. Celita meant a lot to me.

"Good idea! Why not? Get Francisco down here tomorrow."

Celita's anxiety tumbled out like the last air from a deflating balloon, and her smile met mine across the renewed table clatter.

Walking over to the post office, I thought how nice it would be if it were twenty degrees cooler. Suddenly it was. The new brick building had air conditioning. Janice Beecham was the first person I saw when I stepped through the door, and I wished immediately that I hadn't seen her. It was only eleven in the morning and she was pretending not to be drunk. She had dropped her purse on the floor and was on one knee scooping up little runaway items. Two tubes of lipstick would not stay in her grasp. They rolled toward me on the hard, shiny floor, making little clicking sounds. I bent down and stopped their short trip. Janice's red piled hairdo was falling apart. Her sundress was stained with half moons of sweat under her arms. "Hey, slippery little devils, aren't they," I said, as I began to gather some of the other escapees and put them in her purse.

She looked at me as if I were some sort of apparition, then assumed a sloppy familiarity. "Honey, this purse just jumped out of my hand like a frog. That ever happen to you?"

I wanted to put her out of her public misery. "I'm sure it probably has. So, uh, you all set now?" I reached for her arm to help her up. It took her a bit of time to straighten herself. She gripped her purse so hard that her knuckles were white. Her lips were the same. "All set." I watched her maneuver her way out to her car, which I knew she shouldn't be driving. If she crashes, she crashes, I thought, and went to check my mail.

I didn't want to care, but for some reason Janice got to me on an ongoing basis. Anger rumbled in my throat whenever I saw her, with sadness right on its heels. Liking Janice wasn't a consideration. Just the anger, the sadness.

I walked to the hotel to meet Mattie, delighting in the rushing river of anticipation in my veins. Once in the cool hotel lobby, I noticed Carla was in a good mood. She was the Copper Queen Hotel's guardian, the gatekeeper disguised as a desk clerk. You had to go through Carla to get to anyone or anything in the hotel. And she knew just about everything going on in the red-carpeted, proud old building. She motioned for me, so I detoured over to the desk. Out of the corner of my eye I saw Pop sitting on a couch, dark yellow in the dim room's table-lamp light. "Hey, what's up?" I asked Carla, leaning over the desk.

She met my face with a sly grin. "Your girl left you a message." Her hand revealed a neatly folded piece of paper.

"My girl?" I had a sly grin, too. I took the paper and turned my back to Carla to read it. *Kate. Please take Pop to the cafe and meet me at Flagg Pit. Sorry for the switch. MS.* Mattie's initials looked like a cattle brand. I folded the note and put it in my hip pocket. Carla hadn't budged. I slapped the desktop and told her "Thanks."

Pop steadily watched my approach as he sat still in the room's yellow light. His black Stetson took on the shape of a lampshade and his face looked ceramic. "Pop," I nodded a greeting to him. He touched his hat brim, and I pulled him from the clutches of the eerie yellow light. We walked slowly to the cafe in silence, waiting at the cafe door as a skinny man who was talking to himself, or to his imaginary friend, worked up the courage to step onto the sidewalk from the doorway. Pop watched him intently, tuned in to the man's struggle. The man's foot slammed onto the sidewalk, as if it had a life of its own and had just made its first decision. Pop broke into a grin, and as the strange man disappeared, hit my arm and began laughing. He laughed as though it had been years, like rusty barbed wire rubbing against its fence post. I was fixed in time, stuck in my own laugh, unsure, but willing to join Pop wherever he was then. His eyes danced with the scraping rhythm of his laugh. Pop went into the cafe as he wound down to a chuckle. I followed him inside, dizzy from laughing. No one inside had a clue. Just Pop and me.

Only a few cars passed by as I walked on the side of the highway to the pit. As I passed the Copper Queen Mine, I resented its failure, the Copper Queen's final insignificance to the mineral robbers who had to move to bigger and better devastation. The huge open pit mine pushed itself up against the shoulder of the Copper Queen in a constant insult of progress.

Nearing the pit, I wondered where that strange man at the cafe had come from, where he lived, why I hadn't seen him before. Small-town detective. Maybe everyone didn't know everyone after all. Maybe Celita would know. Maybe he lived in Lowell. I rounded the last curve and the edge of the pit came into view. It was dirty blue and yellow and pink, faded in the heat. Layers tapered down out of sight to a bottom of greasy, dead water pools, some red, some black. A giant bucket of mistakes. A true hellhole. An eyesore. A wondrous abyss of human flaw and earthly poisons. And there was Mattie. Perched on a concrete block in the tiny parking lot next to the sign that read *Scenic View*. Gazing out into an ugly Grand Canyon. With her blonde topknot, white T-shirt, dirty white shorts, and bare feet, she looked like a dusty, lost egret. The only other visitor was her black jeep, a big crow perched motionless on its hood.

I came up and squatted by the tall chain-link fence in front of her. She reached down and took my hand.

"I wanted to come out early and look at this thing before we go in the mine. And I'm a little nervous about doing it. Pop OK?"

"Yeah. We had a few laughs."

She gave me a slightly confused, suspicious look, then forgot it. "This is a place I don't understand." Her eyes got lost in the distance down. I turned my head toward the evil, then back to Mattie, waiting. I had already come to know there was always more, but it came a little slowly.

"It must've been something to be a man digging this hole." Mattie got up and walked to the fence, curled her fingers through the chain link, and frowned. The pit had a way of putting visitors in a morose mood. A mood which had no outlet of action, of resolution. There was nothing to do about Flagg Pit. Its hole was there for eternity, poisoned from the possibility of ever becoming something delightful, something romantic to look at like a Seventh Wonder. I had come to terms with the gaping, dead mouth, possibly because it was silent, still, and alone, done but not gone. I never thought of the pit as a grim reminder of what not to do ever again. To me it was a sad ghost, never having had any say about what it was. A naked giant too big to fit into any clothes. An old, dry spittoon. I couldn't imagine being a man digging that hole. I couldn't imagine that hole in the works. It just was. It was always as it was then, with a beautiful windswept horse trainer from Tucson glaring at it as if she could make it wither away from her bitter stare.

I took Mattie's arm and turned her gently toward me. "There's nothing to understand about this place, except that it's dead." The breeze blew her hair to me, and my finger touched her frown.

She looked up from the pavement. "Well, I'm not so sure I want to do this now."

"Let's just get over there and see how it feels."

We drove the jeep back up the road to the entrance of the Copper Queen a half mile away, to the big cracked hill tunneled with dark secrets. The big red-and-yellow sign, *Copper Queen Mine Tour*, turned the atmosphere into a circus sideshow for a brief moment. Billy's taste. Or Janice's.

Mattie was putting her shoes on when I noticed Turrell coming out of the dark gaping entrance. "Here comes Turrell. Let's go." I started toward the entrance. My little scheme was a self-imposed test of my qualifications as guide and bodyguard.

"Kate, wait." Mattie came up behind me quickly, still a little hesitant. "Are you sure this will work?" She looked worried but intrigued.

"Yes. Anyway, it's worth a try. Now come on." Turrell saw us coming and stopped in the middle of closing the chain-link gate. Wednesday was the day he did a little routine maintenance on the train. That's what he called it. From the smell of beer on his bristly face, I think he just did routine maintenance on himself, sitting in there all alone on that silly little empty train.

We had his attention. "So how's that old ghost back there, Turrell? Still kickin' up dirt?" My grin was a twisting knife.

Turrell crossed his arms over his chest and tucked each hand into a dirty, sleeveless armpit. His shirt that day was an oily jean jacket with the sleeves ripped out. His lips were twitching around on his face as he said loudly, "He is. He's still makin' a fuss. Why don't you take a ride sometime and see for yourself?" He looked at Mattie and added, "You and your friend." He seemed annoyed at the intrusion, impatient.

"Well, we just might do that. Is this fella more active certain times of the day? Or is he just wild and unpredictable?" I moved toward the mouth of the mine and gazed into the deep darkness. Turrell fidgeted with the chain and padlock in his hand, struggling with his next move, wanting to leave.

"You never know when you'll see him. Just happens." He was

probably dying for a drink.

"You know, until Billy Beecham started up this train, anyone could go inside. You could walk for a while before you reached the place where it was boarded up. I used to come in here to think. To get some peace of mind. Just sit in the stillness. I loved the smell of the rock, of the dirt. Seemed like the darkness had its own smell, kind of like a ripe berry." This was all true. I looked at Turrell. "Why does Beecham get to lock it up? It's nice in there, isn't it, all by yourself in the dark? Too bad I can't do that anymore." I glanced at the mine entrance and said, "I'd love to show Mattie."

Mattie's voice a few feet behind me claimed, "This is one mine I've never been in."

Turrell was fed up. "He does whatever he wants. I don't fuckin' care if it's locked or not. But he does. If you want to go in there and sit in the dark, go ahead. Maybe the ghost will get you." He looked at Mattie again. I noticed her hard mouth and squinting eyes. "Lock it up when you come out." He tossed the chain and lock toward me. I caught it and didn't make a sound when the padlock swung into my shin.

His boots dragged across the pavement as he disappeared around the corner, knowing their way blindfolded to St. Elmo's. I reached down with a moan and felt the fresh lump on my leg. Mattie touched my shoulder and looked down at my leg, a little excited now. "You OK?"

"Yeah, just a bump." We looked at each other, suddenly realizing my plan had worked.

It was time for phase two. I took the padlock off the chain and closed it with a snap. Mattie drove off with it to the locksmith's with her story. She needed a new key made for this lock. Some fool had dropped her key through a storm drain and she couldn't just buy a new lock because her friend was coming tonight to check on her sick horse for her and had a key to this lock and Mattie was leaving town now for Tucson for a five o'clock flight to Hawaii and didn't have time to take a new key over to her friend's and she didn't want to leave the key out with a note because you never know…. The locksmith would want to shut her up fast.

I went through the gate and closed it behind me. My eyes adjusted to the stretching darkness as I walked slowly alongside the sleeping train. Climbing into one of the empty, open-sided cars, I felt the satisfaction of getting what I wanted. I sat for a while, waiting for my cohort to return with the illicit key. The mine smells came to me, like weary travelers arriving home. I imagined Mattie leaning over and putting her mouth on my neck. As a shiver rattled my spine, I heard the jeep pull up and the engine quit. I met her at the gate, smiling at the shiny new key she held up triumphantly. She came inside, and we wrapped the chain through the gate and snapped the lock shut. The sacred key went into Mattie's deep pants pocket: the Copper Queen was ours.

Mattie tried to adjust to the darkness. "Maybe I'd rather be up in the hills, in the sunlight. I can't see anything," she said. I took a small flashlight out of my pocket. A round, shadowy light appeared on the floor ahead of us.

"Presto! There's your sun. Now relax." We gripped each other's hands and I took the lead. Mattie was tense.

"Relax. Just go slow. This really is a safe place. We won't go too far." I was eight years old and my eyes were bulging, waiting for the elation of the sudden terror that would send me screaming.

"Wait. Let's stop. I just want to stand here for a minute." Mattie was relaxing. She took the flashlight, the little round spot of light drawing shapes all over the walls and ceiling as she explored her dark space. Ahead, the light could not show her the depth of the darkness. "It's hard to get a sense of how far you've gone."

"Well, we wouldn't want to get lost in here. We won't go much farther."

"Where do these tunnels lead? Where does this one end up?" She was touching the rock wall.

"I don't know. It hooks up with another tunnel. And another. There's a lot of them. There's a few different levels, I think. Kind of a subway to hell."

Mattie put the light on my face. I squinted. "You know your way through here?" she asked loudly, looking at me like I was crazy.

"No. I've only been around the bend ahead. You can't hear the highway traffic there." There was no such thing as roaming around a mine. Once you took a couple of turns in the tunnels, it was too easy to get lost. I had never dared to move out of the main tunnel. I had never even gone far enough to find another tunnel. I just liked to sit—blind, enormous, all sense of size distorted, and aware only of my body and its new tomb of cool, heavy air.

Mattie suddenly jerked her head to the right, the spot of light following. "What's that?"

I didn't see anything. It could have been a bat. "Nothing. The darkness plays tricks on you. Let's go around the curve up ahead and sit."

We locked hands and followed the light away from all outside sound, finding a rusted metal remnant of some machine to sit on. I thought to myself that Francisco would probably know his way through these tunnels since he had worked in the mine. We sat in the dark, saving the flashlight for the return trip. Mattie smoked a cigarette, its orange tip drawing an arc from her mouth to her knee and back again. Mesmerized, I watched it, listening to her inhale, exhale. Then it disappeared on the dirt floor. In the sudden, complete darkness, I became very aware of Mattie's presence. I couldn't see her at all and shifted to my right until my shoulder touched hers. She pressed lightly against me. Space became thick inside of me, heavy, bulging.

"Are you afraid?" Mattie's voice surprised me, it was so near.

"No."

"What do you feel?"

"I feel that damn ol' ghost miner—"

"Don't say that!" She sounded serious.

"I'm just kidding! God!" A minute of silence and we settled down. "I feel...full. Of something. I don't know." I let out a hefty sigh and shifted my feet.

Mattie muttered a few words that sounded understanding. Then, in a whisper, she said, "I've never been inside the earth." We were quiet for a while, and the smell of the dirt, the ripe berry, the metallic rock, came to me. I felt the cool air, and somewhere out in the dark a rock or wood beam creaked in its sleep. Then I felt heat as Mattie's hand found my cheek and turned my face toward her. Fingers explored my eyes, my ears, my mouth. The energy filling me snapped like two fingers. Blinded by the dark, in an endless spin there inside the earth, Mattie and I kissed each other. Tugging against tight reins, digging hooves in the earth, mouths quivering, asking for freedom.

I wrapped loving fingers around Mattie's, stumbling over her turquoise ring. Life was pulling me into an ever-bursting intensity in the hands of Mattie Springer. A design of the stars. A twist of fate. I needed to look at her.

"Mattie." My voice was breathless. "I know a creek, up in the hills near here. Let's get out in the sun. I want to look at you. Can we go? To the creek?"

"Uh-huh." It was a gentle hum. "Let's go."

The little flashlight star guided us out of the darkness, and our new magic key let us pass into the sunlight. The hot air spread me out across a plateau of anticipation. I wrapped an arm around Mattie's neck and walked her to the jeep. She tilted her head into my cheek and tried to calm her breath. Our delight soared above us like a giant hawk. The hills to the east waited as we drove up the road to a hidden trail that could not see the world's largest open pit mine.

There was nothing to say in the car, no talk, just the resonance of pounding hearts and thumping tires. We left the car on the side of the dirt road to bake in the sun and disappeared into a line of cottonwoods following a creek through the canyon. The green ribbon split the bare rock walls tilting up on either side of us. Songs of canyon wrens tumbled down from rocky ledges.

Mattie put her hand on the back of my neck as we walked. I felt that anything I would need to know in life from that moment on would be found in the memory of a kiss in a dark mine. The absolutely clear blue sky came through the top of my head and spread through my body. Faraway, the buzz of a small airplane pulled me into the expanse like a drug. There was nothing to say. Nothing to acknowledge. I knew only to do. And Mattie's hand still caressed my neck.

A lizard pulled us off the trail, showing us glimpses of its bright green-and-blue back as it scooted through the cactus and the scrubby sage. We followed it.

"Look down there."

We stopped, and I pointed to the creek. There was a pool out of the current, at the roots of a drooping cottonwood, clear, cool, and protected. We slid down the bank to the sandy creek shore. The world there was different, fresh. The air was cool at our knees, hot at our faces. It buzzed and clicked with insects. Hidden lizards peeked at us, two women in the shade of a lurking passion. A kingfisher darted across the creek, its great beak cutting the sky in two.

I pulled off my T-shirt and stepped out of my jeans. The air on my damp skin excited my breath, pushed my pulse even further. Mattie sat on a rock and watched me slide into the pool and disappear. Under the water I heard the hum of the cosmos. The kiss in the dark came back to me. I swam through specks of submerged sun and tiny waving shadows. When I popped up for air, I saw Mattie's bare legs sliding into the water feet first in front of my face, the edge of her T-shirt floating out toward me as the water rose to her neck. Faster than the kingfisher, her lips were on mine, sure and warm. We danced in the water, unsteady on the slippery rocks below our feet. A silent scream a billion years old finally found its warbled sound. We laughed as we caught our wet breath. "We're going to drown!" I laughed into her eyes and kissed them and said quickly into her ear, "Let's get on land."

The sand was soft and made a bed for me as I lay back into it. My ribs rose and fell with demand as Mattie stood over me, bent her knees, and rested her cool seat on my curly, glistening lap. A new pulse shot through my body like whistling fireworks. Breathless, Mattie pulled off her soaked shirt and paused, taking in the sight of me in my sand bed. I looked up at her wet hair dripping light, her chest calling out for the wind to touch it. Her hands spread across my stomach, moved to gently grasp my sides, then hovered over my breasts as the breeze sang through the passageway between our bodies. I felt her fingers descend softly, surrounding the full moons like a bed sheet floating down to rest on cool night skin. Huge waves reeled against my ribs. Fingers trailed back across my stomach as she looked up at the trees, her open mouth a cave, a mine. The kingfisher glided by above her head. I reached for her, touched her collarbones, ridges above a broad and golden landscape that filled up the sky.

"My, but aren't you tall in the saddle…" My voice disappeared into the sand as my fingers traveled along her body. My pony and I stood on the ridge, looking out over a shimmering desert of buttes and valleys, the rise and fall of the secrets of this ancient land. We walked slowly down to the base of her breast and circled it, climbed up to her nipple and rested our faces against its firm coolness. Then across the smooth plateau we dipped into a valley, rich with forest.

The sky handed down Mattie's face, the landscape tumbled, she kissed me, and we took off at a gallop—outlaws on the run, heading straight for the hills.

6

Back into town, damp and adolescent, we were transformed into a shiny new two-headed snake: there would never be enough. We were late to pick up Pop. A note from Celita on the closed cafe door said, *Pop's at our house.* Now that was an interesting notion, one that left us both speechless. Why didn't Pop just move to Bisbee? I thought. He had lots of new friends. Did he really need us? I wondered why I was irritated. *Because Pop belonged to Mattie and me. He was our creation, somehow.*

"Well, should we go up there?" Mattie seemed at a loss.

"I'm not sure. I guess so. I've never been to Celita's house. It feels weird to think of seeing her in her home. Sometimes you don't want to know too much about a person. You need the rest for yourself."

Francisco's house perched at the top of a cliff overlooking the winding canyon road. Flimsy wooden stairs took us from the car to his door. Catching our breath, we stopped at the top of the steps. I wondered how Pop had handled such a climb. Pointing across the road, I showed Mattie where I lived. "You can see my chimney, there, behind that little blue house."

"So when are you going to show me your house?"

Everything Mattie said ran through my spine like a little mouse.

"Pretty soon, I suppose."

There, above the rooftops, we forgot our feet as our eyes passed through the blue sky like the last few clouds of the day. We forgot where we were until a door opened and a big ugly dog ran to check us out with a couple of barks. Celita was close behind.

"Hey! Thought you disappeared on us!" She seemed either genuinely happy or genuinely intrigued by what could have been rapture leaking from the two-headed snake. "You guys go swimming? Come on in. Hungry?"

We followed Celita inside and into the kitchen. The dog came along. Through the window I could see Pop and Francisco, or the backs of their heads, sitting on the back porch. They didn't seem to be talking, just looking out at the hills and the houses across the canyon. Celita gave us Cokes, and Mattie went onto the porch. I realized I was very hungry, so Celita and I threw together some burritos. We sat at the kitchen table. She watched me as I ate. The back of Mattie's head now appeared next to Pop's and Francisco's through the window.

"Where did you go swimming?"

I felt trapped by Celita's curiosity about my life, as if I had no choice but to answer her questions. I couldn't take my eyes off the three heads lined up on the other side of the window. "Uh, up Lantern Canyon, in the creek."

"You through?" She took my plate and went to the sink. I escaped to the porch.

The sun was moving down toward the red hilltops, the breeze dying. The shade of the porch was ahead of the coming stillness and the quiet of dusk. The old gray wood still showed abandoned, faded turquoise paint from another time. Two worn wooden chairs held Francisco and Pop. Mattie sat next to them on a crate. I moved across from them and leaned against the railing. No one looked at me or acknowledged my presence in any way. Mattie was gazing a little to the south; Pop and his friend stared west, right through me. I wanted to talk, to say something. Whatever it was never came to me, and I felt odd, like a cigarette hanging from a mouth, waiting for a match. The slow, crooked steps of my feet pulled me back through the door without a word.

The living room offered its coziness. I sat on the couch under the watchful eyes of religious statues and framed color photographs of people I assumed were family. Where was Celita? On the porch with the weirdos? The dog came in and squeezed itself between the gold-painted wrought-iron coffee table and my feet. I succumbed to my weary body as it slowly sank with a sigh into the comfort of the couch. Laying my head back, I shut my eyes. Drifting, floating—a particular dusk entered my senses, accompanied by the snoring dog. I took a dreamy ride through the mine again, going further into the tunnel with a huge flashlight. Deeper and deeper, the lightbeam growing larger, radiant.

Voices brought me clearly back into Celita's living room. The dog was dreaming on the floor, his lips and toes twitching, keeping time with a secret rhythm. The voices were coming from the kitchen. Faint accordion music drifted by outside the window on its way back from where it came. I guessed the American Legion Hall. I stood up without waking the dog and sleepily wandered into the kitchen like a little kid stumbling to the table for breakfast in her pajamas. And there was my family greeting me around the table, drinking coffee and eating ice cream. Celita, Pop, Francisco, and Mattie. Every one of them smiling at me.

"Hey, sleeping beauty, sit down and have some dessert. You want tea, right?" Celita needed no answer and was up at a sink full of dirty dinner dishes, rinsing out a cup for me and flipping on the burner under a pot of water. I sat down under the gaze of Mattie's warm eyes reaching for me across the table. A bowl of chocolate ice cream appeared in front of me with a huge spoon sticking up out of it. I made the transition from a slow-motion dreamy world to the cold of the ice cream in my throat, to the renewed conversation at the table, to the remembrance of sex in the sand with a stranger just in town with an old demented gunfighter looking for Wyatt Earp. If I ate my ice cream in silence, I wouldn't blow my cover. Finished, I took my tea and leaned back in my chair, blowing cooling air into the steam rising from the cup.

Celita was finishing a story about the dog. Her face was excited; she seemed very content with her audience. The dog's name was Beano, and he and Francisco had been together for fourteen years. Everyone chuckled into their coffee cups when the story ended. I grinned at the sweetness of it all. Pop's eyes were dancing, and a rivulet of coffee made its way through a tiny canyon from the corner of his mouth down his jaw. Francisco was nodding his smiling head in fond Beano remembrance. Mattie and Celita giggled as Celita got up and cleared the table.

I looked at Mattie, picturing us sitting on my porch when the dusk whispered its plea to turn on the lights inside. As she turned to me, I felt the immediacy of nightfall, the low mourning of the owls. I wouldn't leave her tonight.

Pop stood up as if someone had told him we were going. We were, but how did he know? His gravelly too-loud voice addressed us all. "Tomorrow we'll head out early. Get a good night's sleep, don't drink yourself into a mess." Mattie and I were the only ones who knew what he was talking about, though Celita and Francisco nodded in ignorant agreement.

"Celita, you're great. Thanks." I gave her a tender hug, and Mattie put her arm around her as we walked out. Pop brought up the rear. I think Francisco had gone immediately to bed. I caught a glimpse of Beano by the couch as we reached the door. His head had just popped up from his sleep and he looked slightly embarrassed.

We walked down the stairs, which Pop seemed to know like the back of his hand, and Mattie said, "What a neat kid. She really likes you, made us talk quietly while you were napping."

"Mmm. She's a gift."

I was aware of Pop's hand holding onto a fistful of my shirt as we made our way down the stairs and out into the coming twilight. He sat in the back of the jeep, silent, while Mattie told him we weren't going to the mine tomorrow, that we weren't ready yet. "Kate and I are still scouting. We don't have the layout yet. You've got to give us time." Pop stared out the window at the houses stacked up the side of the canyon.

Mattie pulled up in front of the hotel and told me to wait in the car, that she'd be back shortly. One of the now-familiar waves rolled up my belly to my throat. I watched the two of them walk up the steps and through the door, understanding that their tender backs were protected by Lizzy Springer. About ten minutes later Mattie came out and folded her body into the driver's seat. "I told him I was going to your house." She gave me a serious look. "He said, 'Good. You girls get to work.'"

My house welcomed Mattie with all its heart. It smelled nice, like cedar logs and faint incense. All of my special belongings stood out from their respective places to shout hello. Blue-and-yellow desert rocks, fossils from the sea, skulls and teeth from the prairie, a large tumbleweed, an old beat-up Stetson, a three-foot model of the twenty-mule-team borax wagon from Death Valley. She had to look at everything; I had to look at her. In my house. Under my stars. On my porch kissing me wildly. In my bed telling me that I was her pony and that we were magic. Sending me into the cosmos with her hands and making me cry with her dark eyes. The two-headed snake dreamt, while sleeping, of itself.

7

"I don't want to involve anyone else, Kate."

"It's not involving him—we can't possibly find our way through those tunnels ourselves without getting lost. Maybe he could draw a map for us and not have to go along." I didn't really like that idea as I said it.

"I don't want anyone else to know." Mattie's hotel room was cool. While the sun heated up outside, she sat in a chair by the window and looked out in the direction of home. "I'd like to be able to separate you from this crazy thing. I feel like I'm being haunted. Maybe Pop is a ghost. I want a little sign, some easy explanation of what this is all about. From someone, somewhere." Her voice trailed off into the flat, still heat out the window.

She looked at me and sighed. Her hand caressed my hair as I knelt close to her. "Mattie, just let me ask Francisco if he knows the tunnels. That's all. I won't say anything about why." I wondered if I was making this more difficult than it needed to be.

"I guess we could take Pop in as far as we've been, just past the train, but I don't think that's good enough," she responded.

Through the hotel window, I saw the empty, burning street. "I think we need to get him in the tunnel where that ghost miner is, if we can. And I'm the tour guide, remember?" My eyes narrowed. "I can't be separated from this."

Mattie's hand dropped to her lap as her eyes darted around my face. "You are beautiful. And you're crazy." She got up and looked for a cigarette, her back to me.

"You know," I said, "we can check the Historical Society and see if there's anything there that can help us. We can do that first."

Her *OK* rode out the window on the back of a curl of cigarette smoke and disappeared in the brittle air.

As the sun reached the top of its ascent, Pop and Francisco sat in the cafe, tied to their chairs by Celita's lasso eyes. Mattie and I walked over to the tiny Bisbee Historical Society. The little room of history smelled of weathered, dry pages, with a large, thick wooden table in its center. Three books lay on the table. One was the history of Bisbee. Another was a history in photographs. And the third was the history of mining in Bisbee, which was the history of Bisbee. I sat in one of the six empty chairs around the table and opened the mining book. Mattie headed for the old newspapers. Sarah Nichols, the Society's president, sat behind a desk at the window reading *Gone With The Wind*. She must've been in her sixties; her father had been a manager at the mine. She lived in one of the big houses just outside of town—heavy square shapes so different from the crooked shacks in Tombstone Canyon that twinkled at night like the stars. Sarah lived alone in a large, white, silent house and dreamed the dark secrets of old copper.

I read through the mining book, looking for something about the tunnels that would direct us where we needed to go, a message screaming at me: *If you're taking Pop Walker on a hunt for Wyatt Earp in the mine, follow this map to where the ghost miner lives.*

There was nothing like that. I found out that seven levels of tunnels existed, one hundred feet below each other. Many of the tunnels were flooded because the pumps that were used to keep water out were shut off when the mine stopped its operations. The old photographs in the book were not very clear, but I recognized a mule's face in one. I read that when electricity was installed in the mine in 1921, trains replaced mules for hauling ore out of the mine. The mules had spent so many years in the dark that many of them went blind after they were retired. A sudden sadness made me look up from the book. Overcome with some strange grief for those mules, I tried to force the odd feeling away. I leafed through a section that noted the natural ventilation provided by cracks in the mountain. But I didn't find out anything about the tunnels.

"Kate, look at this." Mattie held the September 1920 issue of the *Bisbee Bee*. "Look at this story." We read it together. "MURDERED MINER SEEKS REVENGE!" The story told about a miner named Jack Timmins who had been found shot to death in Tunnel 3 four months earlier. His murderer had still not been apprehended. Apparently most people thought his rowdy nights in the Lucky Eye Saloon had ultimately caused his death. The writer of the article believed that only the Copper Queen herself knew the grisly story. He went on to say that Raphael Gonzales and Francisco Rivera had seen a ghost in Tunnel 3. Mattie and I looked at each other in amazement. Francisco had seen the ghost!

The description was vivid. They were finishing up repair of a split beam, packing their tools to wait for the train. Suddenly their headlamps flickered and dimmed, and a loud, thundering sound caused them to cover their ears. They saw a large, fuzzy shape ahead of them which turned into a swirling cloud of dust and sped toward the tunnel entrance about half a mile away. When the train finally arrived, their backs were plastered against the wall, their eyes big as boulders with fright. No one believed them. No one else had seen the dust cloud, and a manager interviewed by the *Bisbee Bee* attributed the "imaginings" to too many long hours spent in the mine.

Mattie was out the door, the newspaper dropped on the floor behind her. Sarah Nichols looked up from her book as I pushed my chair back with a screech and bolted after Mattie. I caught up with her across the street. Pop was at the table alone, without Francisco. We sat down with him, and when she was sure no one was paying attention, Mattie said, "Pop, I need to ask you a question." I saw the fright of too many coincidences in her eyes. "I need for you to give me a clear, reasonable answer." Pop's eyes danced. "Why?" Mattie's voice grew loud. "Why do you think Wyatt Earp is trapped in that mine?" His eyes took on that look from another time. He turned away and said slowly, "You know. But you shouldn't, it's not your business."

Mattie put her hands over her face in exasperation and then grasped him by the shoulders. "I don't know! And it certainly *is* my business. If I'm going to take you into that mine, it is my business."

Pop met her harshness by standing up, almost tipping his chair over, and pointing a long bony finger at her face. "We agreed you wouldn't ask." His tone became gentle. "Now Lizzy, you've got to keep quiet." He sat down, took a shaky sip from his coffee, and said to me, "You get us into that mine."

I threw my hands up in the air and looked to the ceiling for help. Mattie stood up and motioned to me. "Let's go."

Pop jumped up. "I'm going with you." He mumbled unhappily as we walked out onto the shaded sidewalk, three pairs of grumpy boots, single file, Mattie in the lead. A thunderhead was building to the north over Buckman Ridge. Our own tumultuous cloud pulled us down the street.

Mattie glanced sharply back at Pop. "What are you mumbling?"

"You two are up to something," he said loudly. "Something. I better keep an eye on you."

Mattie stopped abruptly and swung around in front of Pop. "We're up to something, all right. We're trying to help you find Wyatt Earp in that goddamn mine. But we've got to do this right so you won't get your butt lost in there forever. OK?"

I stepped in. "Some other stuff's come up, and we'd just like all the facts. That's all."

What a stupid thing to say to someone with a leaky brain. Pop stared at me. He was breathing heavily. I didn't know if he was going to keel over or start slugging. He turned to Mattie and said, "You never told me she'd be coming along." He turned with an awkward spin of his boots and walked back to the cafe.

We stood there with our hands on our hips, drawing imaginary lines on the old wooden sidewalk with the toes of our boots, heads bent under the weight of this weird threesome.

"Damn it," Mattie muttered to the sidewalk.

I looked up to the sky with a sigh. "Yeah." A small, lone cloud whisked by hoping not to be noticed. Separated from its tribe, trying to catch up.

"Meet me later?" Mattie said to me. "I think I'll hibernate for a few hours, OK?" She looked a little scared, embarrassed.

"Sure, I'll come down later." I touched her chest reassuringly. "Don't worry." Mattie smiled a smile of defeat. "Don't worry," I repeated.

As easily as the sun disappeared behind the Mule Mountains day after day, a crow landed on the tin roof of Dayton's Feed Store. Stopping my moping boots in their puffs of dust, I looked up to see the crow's straightened black legs dropping in on target. An uncomfortable sensation descended on me as the bird and I stared at each other. The sensation called itself ponderous flight, called itself a shadow. I thought about Mattie counting on me to get her and Pop into the tunnel. The crow cocked its head.

"Well?" I said out loud, half expecting an answer of some kind to come out of its beak. It did. With a few strong pushes of its wings, the crow lifted upward, laughing its name into the low, pink glow of the sky.

I stood in my spot, trapped by the disappearing bird. Someone was coming up the street toward me. I hoped for invisibility. Instead I got Carla in a bad mood.

"That goddamn Jimmy Nunez pitched a cup of coffee at me. Look at my blouse. Now I have to go home and change." Her chewing gum snapped her distress.

"Pitched a cup of coffee?" Jimmy was a quiet busboy, too mild-mannered to be throwing coffee at people.

"Well, he bumped into me with it." She looked at me with new consideration. "What are you doing standing in the middle of the road?"

I hooked my thumbs in my pants pockets and said, "I don't know."

"Good." Carla resumed her disdain and continued down the street. As I watched her trudging home with her coffee stain, it occurred to me that my standing in the middle of the street was no stranger than her walking up the middle of it. Carla knew that she and I had a common command of our street, of our town, and that we could singularly make cars disappear.

The crow was long gone, and I was getting hungry. It was time to put an end to Mattie's hibernation. I remembered that I had promised Celita I would give her a ride to the Beechams' house to babysit.

8

Celita leaned forward from the back of the jeep and plopped her elbows on the tops of the front seats. Her head bobbed between Mattie's and mine as we made our way to the Beechams'. She turned her head to me. "You moving to Tucson?" I gave her a convincing "No." She turned to Mattie. "You moving to Bisbee?" Mattie was silent, watching the road.

"Celita, lighten up." My voice was commanding enough to move her back into her seat. I could feel her pouting.

Janice was standing on her front porch under a yellow light that challenged the dusk. She waved to us from her full, flowered sundress as Celita slammed the car door. I heard cheers from the nearby baseball field as Janice and Celita disappeared into the house.

Mattie turned the jeep around and headed back toward Bisbee. I was trying to imagine Jack Timmins' murder. Wondering where Tunnel 3 was, whether it was full of water. How did the murder happen and how did the murderer get away? The hills grew darker. Through the window I picked out the first planet to light up in the sky. Maybe Francisco knew. Pop wouldn't settle for a brief dip into the main tunnel to have me say, "See? No Wyatt Earp here." He wouldn't be tricked. So Tunnel 3 it would be. If we had to pick a spot, that was the obvious choice. Mattie agreed.

"I told Mr. Randall I'd call him and let him know how Pop's doing." Mattie had told Randall that Pop wanted her to take him to

Bisbee and Agua Prieta, just on the other side of the border twenty miles from Bisbee. She told him they would be gone a few weeks and to save Pop's room. All Randall could do was grumble about not liking her taking Pop. Mattie's explanation of Pop as a friend of her family, mainly of her grandmother, did little to assure Randall of his safety. But Pop had been happy about his trip. He had become rather talkative in the Crystal Palace. "I'm going to the mine," he would say in a low voice. "I'm going to the mine." And to Tombstone's amazement, and discomfort, Mattie had picked up Pop Walker one Sunday and disappeared into the hot southern hills.

"Why don't you call from the cafe? I have a little bookwork to do—won't take long—and we can fix something to eat. I'm hungry." I tossed a steamy look at her. "We'll have the place to ourselves."

She was heartbreakingly beautiful. Her hair danced in the open window's swirl, and the twilight gave her face a mysterious glow. Those burning, smoky eyes looked straight ahead at the road as if she were traveling two hundred miles an hour and one false move would launch her into space.

"Matt, do you ever worry that Pop will get up in the middle of the night and try to go to the mine? My grandfather used to do that. Get up at all hours, leave the house. The sheriff would bring him back, red-faced and angry." It seemed to me now that Pop was teetering on the edge of this wandering world.

"No, he waits. He just waits. Some kind of strange loyalty or something. He always waits for me. Or for you. Because we're all connected. We're connected to that runaway delusion of his. He'll just wait. He knows he needs us to find Mr. Wyatt Earp."

"Who do you think murdered Jack Timmins?" I asked the new night as we pulled up in front of the dark cafe. There was no answer.

The ledger, Tia Tortilla's little secret diary, took my attention while Mattie built a salad and heated tortillas. Looking at all the figures and Celita's receipts gave me a quick flash of homesickness. I wasn't spending much time in the cafe and realized I should check in with Celita tomorrow to be sure she was handling everything all right. I was almost finished when the heavy bowl of towering green plopped down in front of me with a thud. Mattie sat across from me, peering over the leafy hill, demanding something with her eyes. I turned off the adding machine and leaned back in my chair. "What are you thinking, snake eyes?"

The demanding eyes laughed. "Snake eyes...." She took a handful of lettuce and spinach and spread it out on a plate. "A few years ago I was in love with a woman from Montana who had hips like a string bean. Her grandmother called her Snake Hips. She hated that, but I kind of liked it. I had a belt made for her at the State Fair that had *Snake Hips* stamped in the leather. They colored the letters yellow. She liked that belt for some reason." Mattie ate her salad with a mischievous look. I was quiet. I could only imagine Mattie here, now, with me.

Her eyes came back to the present time, looking for me again. "So anyway, I was thinking how incredible it is to be with you."

The sound of crunching salad leaves took over the moment, the room, my brain. I spoke through the clamor. "Maybe after this is done, we can go to the ranch, ride your horses, take a pack trip into the mountains." My words fell flat and spread across the tabletop. The crunching stopped. After what was done? *This* would never be done. *This* was not a task, it was braver than that. This was a rocket vibrating in its launchpad, pointing to the North Star. After a few years in Bisbee, I had come to know that these canyons and these stars could ultimately take anything and anyone for their own. We were spoken for, and we wouldn't be leaving. Somehow I accepted that. And since Mattie ignored my silly words, she must have accepted it too. The rocket would shake in its boots until one day the stars would claim it. And that was that.

"Let's go talk to Francisco tomorrow" was her response.

I got up from the table and said, "I'm full. Finish up the salad, snake eyes," and went to put away the ledger.

"No more for me. Let's just leave it out for Lizzy."

I stopped dead in my tracks. Mattie laughed. "Just kidding. I'm telling you, though, I feel her presence. It's wild. It's like she's always in the next room. Come on. Let's go for a walk." Her hand made a ponytail of my hair as I locked the door, and we turned into the twinkling Bisbee night.

Mattie and I walked a lot. Most of the people we passed in our foot travels greeted us with a nod, others with mild curiosity. We hadn't run into Thea yet. For some reason, we were clear of her, spared from the intrusion of her light-hearted jabs about what life had been like with me. From Turrell we always received a look of suspicion. Pop stared at us a lot, muttering things off and on.

When he was tucked away somewhere, Mattie and I walked the old wooden sidewalks, we walked the trails winding up and down the hills. We walked in the hot sun and in the breezy night. We slept together every night as a matter of enchantment. There was never a question of whether we should. We were old and new. We were magnets for each other. We were hand in hand. I tried to go about business, taking care of my cafe, my house, my inner intrusions, but would ultimately fail, finding myself bouncing in front of a cloud of dust in her jeep, her trusty pony, searching back roads, abandoned mines, each for faraway visions of reason, each for the black spot on the treasure map.

This night, we walked from the cafe up to my house, threw off everything but our shirts, and made love in the hammock. The porch creaked its discontent at being wakened as we swung to the rhythm of the galaxies singing beyond the rooftops. Hammock hobos, stealing our way through ribs and nipples and thighs drawn up tight before spilling into the stars above. Dawn in the hammock came like twilight in a row boat floating on a calm, silver sea.

9

Pop started asking Baby for a whiskey each day after lunch. She finally told him he'd have to go to a bar. One afternoon he got up from his table and went around the corner to the Copper Queen Hotel bar. Mattie and I were sitting on the hotel porch in our usual spot in the shade when we saw him come up the stairs. Mattie jumped up and followed him into the bar. He ignored her. "He just sat at the bar and ordered his whiskey," she reported as she returned to her chair next to me. It was like he was home, in the Crystal Palace. And that became his new routine after his long lunch in the cafe: having a couple of slow whiskeys in the bar.

It wasn't long before he started demanding to go to the mine for Wyatt. "Get the guns, we're going in," he would say, his voice low and shaky. Mattie finally took Pop on Turrell's train tour with the hope of appeasing his restless desire to search the mine for Earp. I wouldn't go. I couldn't associate with the hated train, or Turrell. While I'd certainly heard about the tour, I'd never been on it, and I had a slight concern that Pop would do something weird when he got in the mine. What would he be thinking, looking at the passing rock walls and listening to Turrell? I wondered how Pop would handle it all.

While they rode the train, I lay on my couch, staring into the past two weeks. It seemed like two lifetimes since Mattie had first walked up the steps to the Copper Queen Hotel. Images of Mattie's close face, coal eyes, and teasing smile flew past me like a crow, cawing to be noticed. Scenes of dark tunnels and beams of light thrown from flashlights danced around me. My hands could feel her hips, the tight lean muscles of her arms and legs, the softness of her hair, of her golden belly. I felt the excitement—this lover of mine was striking gold all over me. The lightheadedness that lifted me by my hair into the sky was my nightly companion. My canyon-top perch poised me for the daily leap into Mattie's body, and into the mysterious mine.

I could feel the heat creeping in under the door; it was time to pull the house's south-facing shades. But the couch held me until the phone rang.

"Cactus Kate."

"Why do you still call me that?" It was a dead name.

"Listen." Thea was so irreverent. I suddenly had no memory of our years together. "You're never home anymore. I've been trying to call you for days. So who is this woman you've suddenly taken a shine to?"

A shine? I liked the way that sounded. *Thank you, Thea.* I softened to this whip of a visitor. "Mattie."

"I know. Why is she here with Pop Walker?"

"They're friends. They're on vacation together." This was amusing. "How've you been?"

"It's like you dropped off the face of the earth, Katie."

I liked the sound of that, too. "I'm around."

"You're never in the cafe. I stopped by a couple times to tell you that I found a bronze horseshoe clock. Didn't Baby tell you? It's in that secondhand store in Sierra Vista and it's only thirty-five dollars."

"Did you get it?" For years I'd wanted one of those. Thea would never forget what I wanted, who I was, where I'd been. It was easier to remember in such a small town. She would be the expert on me always. But now I was sneaking by her undetected, unknown, as I headed for the stars with Mattie.

"No," Thea said. "I didn't have enough money on me, but I gave the guy a ten and he's holding it for a while. I'm going back next weekend if you want me to pick it up for you."

I did. Thea told me it should sit on top of the cash register in the cafe, and she said Baby agreed. So that was that. I told her I'd try to bring the money by in the next few days, but declined a dinner invitation for me and the woman I'd taken a shine to. As I left for the cafe to meet Mattie, the heat and Thea's generosity walked down the canyon with me, falling behind and then catching up, like a distracted little kid.

Francisco was with Pop at their table, the noon ritual. I sat down and smiled at them, but only Francisco smiled back. Pop was mumbling discontentedly out the window. Celita waved to me from behind the counter. Baby must have been smoking in the bathroom.

Mattie came in, smiling a nod my way as she sauntered up to the counter. Celita gave her a soda and they chatted for a few minutes, probably about Celita's evening at the Beechams'. Their favorite subject. Even though she hadn't met Janice, Mattie was enthralled by Celita's stories about her, stories much more enthusiastic than mine. Mattie came over to the table on the tail end of a shared chuckle and pulled up a chair. "Well, how's it going fellas?" Her smile turned to me, and I felt her hand cup my knee. "Kate."

The greeting came straight from the dark of her eyes and landed in my lap. I glanced at the two old men, feeling on my face the look of power that comes from being part of two. They had stopped eating and were both looking at us, waiting for our next move. I was wondering what had happened during Pop's train ride, whether Turrell had pointed out the ghost tunnel. I asked Mattie.

"The train tour was weird, I thought. I'm not real sure what Pop thought of it." Mattie threw a glance at Pop and he turned his eyes away. Enough said, I guess. "Janice bought a bird," Mattie continued. "A parakeet." Mattie's chuckles resumed. Celita told Mattie that Janice named the bird Koko. Janice had made Celita watch while she threw Koko kisses from her lips. They sounded like rapid drips from a leaky faucet. The bird responded with love chirps. Janice warned Celita not to take Koko out of its cage. Celita didn't like the bird because it squawked in competition with the television. She thought it might stop if she let it out of the cage. But Celita knew that if Janice found out she gave Koko a taste of freedom, she would fall to pieces. And Celita didn't want that to happen.

"Celita's right." I knew. "Janice has something of her own now, something nobody else better mess with."

Francisco was nodding his head in agreement. I leaned on my elbows toward him across the table. "I read a story about you in an old newspaper, Francisco." Pop turned his gaze to his table mate. Francisco seemed embarrassed as he shuffled his feet under the table and smiled into his lunch plate. "In 1920. It was a great story," I continued with a bit of a smile. "I'd like to hear more, about what it was like to see that ghost." I gave him a tender look. "You've probably got lots of stories. Do you tell Celita? Stories need to be passed on, you know."

"That ghost. No one believed us."

His voice cracked through the air like twigs being stepped on. I was surprised that he took the risk to speak. I had expected to have to try to coax a response out of him. These two guys were both carrying lots of surprises in their hip pockets. He stopped with those words. I imagined him long ago, shunning the ridicule, the teasing, burying the event in the back of his life, wishing he had never told a soul.

The twigs snapped again. "Raphael died in that mine. Too careless after the ghost."

Pop's face contorted at Francisco's words, becoming startled and scowling at the same time. His eyes sharpened like two new pencils.

"He was the only person who believed you." Mattie's matter-of-fact voice interrupted Pop's ensuing mumble, but not before I picked out "murder" from his tumbling words. Francisco was nodding as he resumed his lunch. He looked up at me as I asked him to tell us what it was like that day in the mine. I wanted to be there. He didn't respond one way or the other.

Mattie changed the subject. "How long did you work in the mine?"

His face hardened, and he answered slowly. "Over twenty years, anyway. Until it closed in 1939. Then I worked the pit."

"Think you could still find your way through all those tunnels?"

He was finished eating and took a few long gulps from his Coke. "It's done, that mine. It kills." The empty can went back to the table with a loud *ting,* which seemed to unsettle Pop even more.

Mattie and I watched them both, in their silence, two parallel universes. Francisco's stare traveled out the window and across the street. The juice of Pop's lunch crept down his chin. My body flattened out in the chair with a heavy sigh. Now what?

"Forget it. Forget it, for now." I sat across from Mattie on her bed, watching her smoke a cigarette. Her hand dangled from her arm as it rested on her upright knee as the smoke wound its way past her dreamy, worried eyes and out the window. The little lamp on the bedside table struggled to light up the space between us. I reached comfortably for her leg and tucked my fingers in the angle behind her knee. "Don't worry about it," I said gently.

"Francisco won't go in the mine," Mattie said as she smashed her cigarette out in the ashtray, making the bed jiggle. "He won't even talk about it now. And the train doesn't go in that tunnel. Turrell won't say where it is. This is getting crazy."

"No it's not." I put my arms around her.

"Yes it is, goddamnit." Her voice turned into short sobs, and she pressed her face into my neck.

Her eyes dampened my skin as I closed my eyes with the sweetness of it. "Mattie." I spoke in a low, sure, unfamiliar voice. "It's OK. We'll do it. We're all set. We just need to stumble on the right road. It's there. We don't need Francisco. This isn't crazy and you're not crazy and I'm going to get us in that tunnel. It's OK." My voice stopped as I felt her kissing my neck. Her breath caught up with the last remaining sobs and her mouth snuck up to mine. A giant spring snapped in my chest. She shifted around and sat in my lap, gathering me in her long, bare arms and wrapping her legs around my hips. I heard her say my name, half question, half exclamation, as we jumped head first into each other's eyes.

I was wound around her later like a ball of string, naked to the night, heavy with the calm of giving up myself. Two huge stones, unmovable. Breathing one breath together. Inside my legs was the memory of her hand staking out territory, looking in the dark hollows for more land. The memory of my hair traveling along her skin behind me as I looked for the deep, low glow lurking around every curve.

I squirmed, and she tightened her sleep grip. *Don't move. We are soaring now, don't let go don't let go.* We were in the same position when the morning light woke me. I shifted slightly and fell back to sleep.

Mattie startled me with her clear, awake voice. "Pop didn't say one word during the train tour. Not one. He stared straight ahead. I couldn't say anything because I thought he was somewhere else and whatever I would say would probably be incomprehensible, or stupid. I don't know if he even heard Turrell's voice telling us about the ghost."

"Maybe he's never been on a train, even a little electric one. Maybe he was in shock," I mumbled.

"I don't know, but that was a weird train ride. Not like really riding in a train. More like a little red wagon. We squeaked and jerked through the tunnel, and the loudspeaker buzzed whenever Turrell talked over it. No one said a word to each other. Not a word about the tunnel, no questions. There were six other people, looking pretty uncomfortable, holding on for dear life going two miles an hour.

And Pop. Staring straight ahead like he was really going somewhere." Mattie got dressed. "No wonder you've never gone on that tour. I looked at the dark rock, broken every few yards by a light bulb. Small, silent secrets laughing their sparse light. I asked out loud, 'How old is this rock?' No one answered me. No one noticed me." She pulled on her boots. "Well, I guess the light bulbs did."

We ate breakfast in the hotel dining room among the sideways glances of several other couples. I blurted out, "Monday is my birthday." I loved my birthdays. Mattie's scrambled eggs fell off her fork, short of her mouth, and she stared at me over it all.

"Next Monday?" The words creaked out of her mouth.

"Yes. Why are you being so strange?"

"So's mine." It came out slowly, and she let the fork go back to her plate. "Nineteen fifty-seven."

"*Nineteen fifty-seven.*" My mouth dropped open and delight jumped into my eyes. "Mattie, we were born on the same day!"

Mattie put her face in her hands and said, "Jesus."

I slapped my hands together and let out a reverent, "Whoa!"

Mattie peeked at me through the open fingers covering her face and said, "You're not kidding?" I didn't need to answer that.

"OK." I asked the final question. "What time?" I stretched my face toward hers until it was a few inches away. Her hands dropped to the tabletop, and she gave herself over to her answer. "Noon."

"Noon!" I laughed. "I was born at midnight!" We stared at each other. In the midst of this wonderful discovery a breath of relief touched my heart at the twelve-hour difference—a reminder to the two-headed snake that we were separate people after all, that we could step back and look at each other, then step forward and take each other in.

Mattie was speechless. I told the waitress. I told two senior citizens at the table next to us, two women whose pink lipstick stretched a mile for us. Jumping up from my chair, I squeezed Mattie's face between my tingling hands and gave her a loud kiss on the lips. She began laughing, and I fell back into my chair, trying to drink my coffee with trembling hands. Maybe all those times in my life when I had felt utterly alone I hadn't been alone after all. In one brief morning over scrambled eggs, the horizon of my life took on an entirely different look to me—a new hue, a new pull, a thicker line.

10

The key clunked in the padlock as I slipped off the dull metal chain. We darted through the gate before the next car came by on the highway. The coolness of the mine touched our faces, and the train slept, unconcerned with our presence. Outside, the sun's brightness faded the road and hillside to a faint yellow-white.

Our birthday had dawned crisp and definite. The morning felt slightly pressured, enticing us to notice everything—the fine line between the red ridges and the brightening blue of the sky, the sound of the wrens, the smell of each other. Mattie gave me a small silver horseshoe pendant, telling me that luck and beauty made the perfect companions. I delved into my collection of found objects and presented her with a perfect hawk feather to which I tied a leather thong and a tiny bell. She attached it to her rearview mirror in the jeep. Our big present to each other would be a foray into the mine. We would find a clue. We would be sure not to get lost. We would go a little further than the first time, and not be afraid. We left Pop at his table with Francisco. "It's our birthday," we told him. "We're going scouting in the mine. Don't tell anyone. It's our birthday secret." He looked at us with narrowed eyes and said, "Keep quiet." That sent us off with no further words.

"I wish we could turn on the lights. Are you sure they'd be noticed from the road?" Mattie scanned the electrical switches with the flashlight.

"If Turrell goes by, he'll notice. That's all we need, is for him to find us in here having sex in his train!" We hadn't come to the mine to have sex, but it was our birthday and the notion quickly came to mind. We paused in a stare, and then Mattie laughed.

"Come on." She led the way and I followed, pretending that she would go straight to our tunnel. What had I been worried about, anyway? We decided that we could at least follow the main tunnel without turning into side tunnels, except to peek. As we walked, little jerky steps sending up puffs of dust, the darkness intensified until it became a voice telling me I was an astronaut entering a new universe and that I had better watch out. Suddenly, Mattie inhaled a short scream. We both hit the dirt. The sound of wings and stirring air circled above us as the flashlight found a few upset bats. We huddled in the dirt until they moved on to settle elsewhere.

"We should have thought about bats," Mattie whispered. My heart had dropped into my legs. And over a few bats. Meeting a ghost in this mine, I guessed, would be the end of me altogether.

Wiping the dirt off our pants, we followed the flashlight with resolve. I tried to keep my eyes intent on the round light just ahead of me, my hand tight in Mattie's. But the darkness began to come alive. I was scared to death and couldn't even say so.

A new smell invaded the ripe air. A smell of sweaty hair. And I thought I heard hooves scraping off the edges of small rocks with every other step. Then I knew it was a mule. I felt sweat on my forehead even in the cool air, sweat on the mule's flanks. I heard voices in the distance, men grunting, and the heavy clank of metal ax against rock. I thought I saw the mule in front of me, life fading behind me. We grew to enormity and filled the hill and all its tunnels. I smelled the leather harness, the dirt, the cool sweat, the rock, the blindness. My heart ached, my hands hurt. I thought I would fall backward like a huge boulder off a cliff.

Mattie's voice sliced through the thick vision, and it fell, lifeless, in the dirt. "I hear water dripping." She stopped and I bumped into her. My eyes were crying without tears. I was afraid of what had happened to me. What came out of my mouth was not what I really wanted to say.

"There's always a little water seeping down from somewhere in a mine. Always dripping somewhere off in the distance." How did I know that? Maybe everyone knew that. I wanted to tell Mattie to hold on to my hand tighter, because I was slipping through a crack in time.

"Yeah, I remember I saw some wet rock from the train, but you can't hear anything but the train." She began walking again. "Pay attention. Look for tunnels." I guess I hadn't been. My awareness pulled the layers of present time back over itself: a dead mine, a small round light, a strong hand gripping mine. I swallowed my frightened imagination. The dripping water stayed in the distance, and we walked slowly toward darkness, scanning the rock walls for an opening. Finally it was there, on the left. We stopped and shined the light into its gaping black mouth. No train tracks. It was timbered, and what appeared to be a pile of fallen rock partially blocked the way a few yards past the entrance. We walked in to get a better look. The pile seemed easy enough to get around. "Maybe that's the worst of it, huh?" Mattie said, scanning the rocks with her flashlight.

"I doubt it." Keeping a grip on caution, I turned us back into the main tunnel and we continued. The ceiling got a little lower, and we heard a new, closer dripping. Our trusty light showed us the wet sheet of water to our right covering a high shiny dark slab of rock—like sweat on a mule's flank. Slow drops disappeared from the slab and into cracks below it. We followed the train tracks a few more yards and came to another tunnel, this one larger than the first and without any obvious obstacles. The tracks switched off into the tunnel. We followed them without a word, through debris, wooden crates, rusted pieces of machines, old flattened garbage, the dull broken glass of bottles. I sat down on a crate and said, "Now, it's OK to do this, but one turn off from the main tunnel only. As a matter of fact, we stop here."

Mattie looked around with the flashlight. "I'm not going anywhere." But she walked a few steps toward something the light didn't quite understand. "What's that?" I got up to look. We both inched closer to a place where the wall seemed to have disappeared. It was like a shallow cavern. The tracks continued into the darkness as we explored the curved cavern wall. Miners had scooped out this elegant place, and we were stepping into it years later. The rock was different here. Light streaks traveled through it, following hard blues, reds, and greens. I felt like I was in the middle of one of those rocks that are split open to reveal a world of glistening purple crystals. We sat in the dirt with our backs to our find. "It's shaped like a big horseshoe. Horseshoe Cavern." I named it.

I remembered the history book—the mules. "Let's turn off the flashlight," I said to her. Now we were blind. Blind with the mule ghosts. My sweat began to cool; fear began to fade away. I heard nothing. No water, no stirring. No creaking wood. No mule breath, no hooves. I had no body, just my heart, sitting in the dirt alone, beating.

After several minutes Mattie whispered, "I'm going to turn on the flashlight." The light gave me her face, our birthday, and her shimmering eyes. I held on to her tightly, there in the cavern of the mule. The light pointed directly above us, and as we stood up, it turned around to the cavern and rested on the shape of a person. I stumbled in place. Mattie's hand flew to cover her mouth as tears leaked from her eyes. I saw a faint face, a woman with long, light hair, her body in trousers and boots and a white dirty shirt, a hat in her hand. She was there only for a few seconds, and then the wall took her into itself. My head was clear; the light was clear. The air teemed. The tiny birthday horseshoe rested lightly against my skin under my shirt. I stared into the empty light and heard Mattie crying. I put her face into my hands. "It was Lizzy, wasn't it?"

She nodded and kept crying. A cry that was soft and too new to reach into its depths. Excitement grew in my bones and flashed in the top of my head.

"Let's go." She gave a whisper, the kind that finishes a cry, and we walked carefully back to the main tunnel, turning in the direction of unseen daylight. We had seen Lizzy. I would repeat that over and over in my head the whole day. Never mind Jack Timmins. Now this made two ghosts to contend with. Maybe more—I wondered if Mattie had felt the mule, too, but I couldn't ask.

Mattie rubbed her damp nose and sniffled as we moved away from the confounding event. I stepped on something in the dirt and stopped. "Wait." I took the flashlight and pointed it at my boot. I stood on a hat, soft and smashed, powdered with dirt. Mattie bent slowly to pick it up. She brushed the dirt off and tried to give it back its shape. A gray Stetson. Old. Her hands caressed it for a minute, then she put it back in the dirt, a little behind a rock against the wall, away from the tracks. Without a word, we went on. There was no need to say what we both realized. It didn't matter if the hat had been there unnoticed on our way in. It didn't matter. We both knew it was Lizzy's. It was Lizzy's hat.

11

The moon was up, a quarter full, looking at us through the windowpane next to our table in the hotel bar. The old glass distorted the crescent shape, turning it into a large, white peanut shell. I tilted my head up and down to change the shape at will while Mattie and Janice chatted. I wasn't too pleased that Mattie had accepted Janice's loud invitation to join her at her dark table; she finally got to meet the subject of many conversations with Celita. Janice was without Billy. Apparently she no longer depended on his presence to go out to drink. I was mesmerized by the shape-shifting peanut moon and the low Mexican music in the bar. Janice's voice broke the spell.

"...not enough business. I told him he ought to let me drive it—get rid of that nasty Turrell Fisher. I could wear my flower-print overalls. And a miner's hard hat. And I would liven up those silly stories."

Mattie jumped in. "We could reenact the dead-miner ghost story. Kate and I could hide in the dark in one of the tunnels and throw handfuls of dust out and make ghost sounds."

Janice frowned. "I think Turrell made that one up."

They giggled. I said, much too seriously, "No he didn't. So, business isn't so good these days?"

Janice looked at me as if she'd forgotten I was there. Her giggle faded. "Well, no," she said, unsure if this was a serious enough answer. Then she snapped her fingers in front of my face. "But I was telling Mattie that I could make business pick up real quick."

I glanced out the window. The moon was hiding behind a traveling night cloud. If Billy stopped running the train, we wouldn't have to share the mine. And that horrible red-and-yellow sign could come down. I looked at Janice. She'd stopped talking and was grooming the glowing orange coal of her cigarette against the side of the ashtray. Mattie stared at me with piercing eyes, slowly smoking her cigarette. The break in conversation was uncomfortable for Janice.

"Ronnie hates my bird," she confided, "and Billy won't let me drive the train. He won't even come for a drink with me."

"You need an adventure." Mattie put out her cigarette with her words.

I cocked my head to the side. *What adventure?*

"Yes I do. I need an adventure." Janice laughed awkwardly, looking to Mattie and then to me for help. Now she was lost. Time to go. I stood up. "Midnight. I'm sleepy. Time for me to hit the hay."

Suddenly Mattie had to hit the hay too, and Janice seemed to know why. "You girls are cute." It slipped out before her embarrassment could stop her. Mattie put her hand on Janice's shoulder and said, "Good night, hotshot."

Janice was smiling as we left her and wandered into the sleepy lobby of the hotel, the bar noises fading behind us. We walked together up to Mattie's room.

"You really like her, don't you?" My hand slid softly up the worn wooden railing as we climbed the stairs.

"Yeah, something about her." Mattie said she thought Janice was a fringe dweller, a true misfit hiding under the mask of vodka, lipstick, and a sundress, and that one day, probably soon, she would lose all interest in vodka and emerge an enlightened madwoman to whom we should listen.

I hoped so. But I could wait. "So what kind of adventure do you think she should have?"

"Something hot and sweaty. And dangerous." Mattie smiled at the thought.

When we got to her room we had our own hot and sweaty adventure, running wild through folds of sheets and fat pillows and brass bedposts. Just before sleep, I noticed the small round shape on the ceiling, an unobtrusive glass globe that covered the darkened light bulb behind it. It watched us in stillness. My eyelids began their descent into sleep, and the round ceiling eye flattened into an old smashed hat in the dirt on its way out of my sight. Sleep brought me a dream that would follow me in dark silence, just out of reach of my memory. In the dream, a huge old mule, dead, with translucent eyes, was falling through the sky, slowly. It turned graceful cartwheels, flinging its legs like a rag doll, floating on its back, head over heels, silent. Then four horseshoes dropped from its hooves and fell heavily to earth.

12

My nipples were little ten-gallon hats. They stood tall at rest. And when Mattie visited them, they reached for the sky. They sang soft old cowboy ballads to her as she spread her bedroll under their moon shadows, sighing into the last burning embers of her campfire. And when the sun rose and long bands of gold inched across the plateau, they watched her sleeping face turn gold.

"Kate!" Mattie's urgent voice startled me out of my cartoon fantasy. I sat up in bed and looked out the window for the time of morning. Late. And hot. Mattie must've been up for a while, and I hadn't even known it. Now she was standing at the foot of the bed, staring at me as if I was suddenly unbelievable.

"I'm up," I said as I moved the sheet off my legs. "I'm up. How long have you—"

"Pop's gone."

This declaration silenced me, and I sat frozen with one leg out of the sheet. We stared at each other for a horrible moment. Then I asked, stupidly, "Where?"

Mattie's legs folded, and suddenly she sat on the floor with a thump. Her hands thrashed through the air as she cried, "I can't believe it. I should never have done this. What am I going to do? We have to look for him. How can I tell people he's disappeared? God, I can't believe this!"

This was not going to happen. Pop had not disappeared as if he had never happened, as if Mattie had never happened, as if whatever was in that mine was not there. I stretched over the end of the bed, reaching for her shoulders. "Mattie! Mattie, stop. We'll find him, he's around. It's not like he hopped a plane, or hitched a ride with a trucker. He's got to be right around here. We'll find him." I forced a nod from her. "Let me get my clothes on." I was dressed in thirty seconds except for one hiding boot. "We're going to find him," I grunted, as I pulled the boot out from far under the bed.

I steered the jeep straight to the mine. Mattie bit her nails, looking ahead farther than she could see. I tried to get some information from her.

"Was Carla there? Did she see him leave? Did anyone see him leave the hotel?"

Mattie couldn't answer.

"Breathe," I told her firmly as the jeep screeched into the parking lot and stopped just short of the entrance to the Copper Queen. The morning tour was just loading. We arrived in time to see Pop getting on the train. Mattie dropped her face into her hands. When she moved to get out of the jeep I put my hand on her arm, stopping her, and said gently, "Let him go. He's OK."

She relaxed into my hand. "I wonder if he thinks he's going to come back out of there with Wyatt Earp?"

"I think he just likes that little train." I tuned to a country music station and opened my door to any breeze that might happen by. "Maybe the darkness and the smells are sending him some messages. Something's knocking on his door."

My eyes closed as I let my head slip back on the seat. Maybe he would find Lizzy's hat. Maybe he would see Jack Timmins' ghost today. I smelled Mattie's cigarette and felt the jeep move slightly as she leaned against it outside. I went on a lonesome trip with the slide and twang of the music, to someone else's pain, someone else's highway. I could see with my closed eyes skinny pine trees zipping by, Confederate flag license plates. My mother's mourning voice singing next to me in the car wrapped a fist around my heart. I thought to turn the radio off, but I couldn't. A few minutes later I opened my eyes to see Mattie leaning through my open door, looking at me, her face a bright ball of western sun hanging in the wide open space. I touched her face. "You OK?"

A steady "What are we going to do?" was her reply.

"We're going to ask him how the mine's doing and then we're going to take him to the cafe."

"He's going to come here every day," Mattie said, worried.

"Yeah." I got out of the car and stretched my still sleepy limbs to the cloudless sky. "Maybe." The highway winding down the desert hills boasted no Confederate plates. The sun's hot breath blew up from the soft asphalt into my face as I made a silent request for some cool shade and a non-demented Pop Walker. Neither existed.

As we waited for the train to return, I wondered if it was good that Pop would come to the mine every day. It could be, but he'd never remember what days it was open for tours. I pictured his stick figure walking along the highway to the mine and wondered what had been in his head, what teeming anticipation. As always, I was impressed with his stamina; he looked so frail.

We were running out of things to do with him in this pause while we tried to figure out how to find our way into Tunnel 3. Mattie found Pop up and dressed by seven-thirty every morning, sitting on the side of his crumpled bed. Sometimes she'd take him to the barber for a shave. Sometimes she'd talk him into putting on his spare set of clothes and take him with her to do his laundry—once in a while you'd see Pop in a white shirt instead of his usual black one. Most of the time I was there, too, knowing I should probably be spending more time at the cafe, but it was hard to keep away from them.

I found myself thinking it was wrong to make him wait unnecessarily, that we should get moving on finding the tunnel. Meet the murdered miner Jack Timmins. Introduce him to Pop. Maybe introduce him as Wyatt Earp. I had to come up with a new idea. I wondered if Pop's plight was now just a cover for these two whirling dust-devil lovers. Time to pick it up. Remember the hat. The hat was a beginning, and we had left it as an end. It was still there. We weren't.

I turned to Mattie in the blazing parking lot. "It's a good idea. If he comes here for the tours, it might help satisfy some of his frustrations. Give him some control."

Mattie wasn't so sure. "What if he tries to get off the train and walks into one of those tunnels?"

That was a possibility. Pop's delusion was set in concrete. If we got him into the tunnel, and there was no Earp, he'd still believe the dead marshall was in that mine somewhere. Pop's mind would know no end to the tunnels; there would always be more. Tunnels off into other universes, endless entrails encompassing several realities, like his brain. But I believed something would happen by taking Pop into that tunnel with the murdered miner's ghost. Something that would set him free.

"Well, if he gets off the train, I certainly hope Turrell would retrieve him. Let's see what he did in there today." I looked deeply at Mattie. "You know we've got to get back in there." As soon as I'd said it, I heard the train approaching from the dark mysteries of the tunnels. Mattie crossed her arms and fixed her eyes on the entrance.

Pop was the last person to come out. Turrell was walking beside him, holding his arm, a little too tightly I thought. Pop's face was hard. Turrell deposited Pop a foot in front of me, crammed his big dirty hands onto his hips, poked his face out at me, and spit out his angry words. "Your little buddy ain't going to ride my train any more. He's crazy." Pop turned his face away, his lips moving in silence.

"Turrell, you're an asshole." The last time I had called him an asshole was a couple of months ago when he came in the cafe one day and started harassing Celita. I had walked up to his table and took his food away from him, told him an inch from his face to never set foot in my cafe again, and went to the phone and called the sheriff. For a while I was worried he would wreak some horrible revenge on me. But it turned out that he was too stupid, and usually too drunk, so he just took delight in being nasty to me.

"What's your problem?" I continued. Turrell's eyes narrowed, forcing a drop of sweat from each eyebrow. "Do you know who this old gentleman is? This is Pop Walker, and I know you've heard of him. You don't talk like that about him, OK?" I gathered myself and shed my angry edge. "Now think about this. You've got a famous gunfighter from Tombstone on your train. Tourists come to see him in the Crystal Palace. So he's a character, a little bit off—delightfully so, I think—so what? People love him. Only someone like you wouldn't. Catch a clue, Turrell. You've just been handed a way to liven up your tour and maybe increase business. Talk it up, fool." What was I saying? My mouth had no brakes.

Mattie confused Turrell with a little chuckle, and he gave her a quick stab with his eyes. Pop looked at him, waiting, knowing it was Turrell's move in this apparently touchy game. Turrell's voice rolled through gravel as he said, "He talked to himself the whole time. Made people uncomfortable, talking loud, and it was all nonsense. People stared at him. He interrupted my legends. I don't care who he is. He's crazy, and I don't want this old shit on my train." He backed up a few steps and pointed a finger at me. "You're crazy, too, hanging around with him. What are you doing with him, anyway, two queers and a senile old man?" I shot a glance at Pop. He had a look on his face like he was about to say, "What's a queer?" Turrell sneered at us as he turned back toward the big black hole in the rock. Several tourists were frozen at their car doors, captivated by the odd parking lot drama in this ghostly mining town at the edge of the stars.

The County Office of Mining and Geology was in a tilting wooden building next to the courthouse in Lowell. It smelled of dust; its old floors dipped in critical places. I was told that the county wouldn't release any operations information to a private party. Neither would the Copper Queen Consolidated Mining Company. Mattie didn't seem surprised. So we were stuck. Again. Maybe when we went back in the mine, I thought, the hat would be in a new place each time, until eventually it landed in our tunnel.

I waited for a couple of days for a new idea to come, trusting completely that it would. It did.

"I know what adventure Janice needs." My announcement came from the doorway behind Mattie on my afternoon porch. She looked around to see my slightly serious, bragging face. I was quite pleased with my idea.

I sat down next to Mattie, facing her. She waited in silence. A hummingbird appeared suddenly in front of us, checking us out, then zoomed off in astonishment. The sound of its humming wings seemed to linger behind it for a brief moment. "Aren't hummingbirds supposed to be good luck in China?" Mattie spoke to the now vanished hum.

"Yes, in China," I replied, "and in Bisbee." We relaxed into the worn, welcoming wood of my porch steps, and I explained my new idea.

13

The high sun lit up Janice's orange hair as vagrant wisps twirled free of the beehive configuration. Her fake eyelashes cast dark shadows down her cheeks. She looked painted for war. Why would anyone wear false lashes on a 110-degree hike? Her upper lip twitched under beads of sweat—sweat that smelled of powder and perfume, unwelcome guests in the hot desert air. Her pasty white arms glared at me. They had no muscle tone, none. I remembered Mattie saying to me, "That's my favorite thing about her. Those cylindrical arms, no muscle, no boniness. They're so unassuming."

"What are you looking at, you strange girl?" Janice's voice was oddly low and drawn.

"Your lashes, Janice. Never noticed them before. Must be the light." I smiled stiffly.

Mattie came out of the hotel door onto the porch where Janice and I stood. "Hey! Ready to roll? You look great Janice. New jeans?" She kissed my cheek and hopped down the steps. Stopping there and looking back up at us, she said, "Let's go for God's sake."

Janice and I stood staring down at her, unable to bounce into the world as she had just done. We seemed fixed in the shadows of Janice's lashes, bound by the black lines to a fear of the unknown. I wasn't sure why I felt so strange and was quickly trying to figure it out when Janice did a really odd thing: she reached both hands up slowly to her eyes and peeled off her lashes. Then she dropped them on the porch. The black lines were gone, and we were free to move down the steps to my waiting Calamity Jane. As we walked away, I worried that someone would slip on those lashes and break their neck.

Janice kept the pace slow, and I felt her stifled whining. We were headed up Buckman Ridge. Mattie carried lunch in her pack.

"You should see this place at night, Janice. All the stars make you feel like you're about to topple off the edge of the world." Mattie was in a great mood. Shining.

"I feel like that most of the time, and it's not pleasant." Janice spoke down to the path. I put my hand on her bare flaccid arm and said, "You're getting sunburned. Mattie, did you bring sunscreen?" They both ignored me.

"Janice, you probably feel that way because you don't look up in your life." Mattie was dynamite in Janice's heart.

Janice scrambled to say something cute. "You—well don't think looking up is going to keep you on the road, missy."

Mattie smiled and dropped it. I knew Janice was going to die of sunstroke on that path within an hour if something wasn't done. I tried again.

"Anyone bring any sunscreen?"

Janice answered me curtly. "I am not getting sunburned. I put my sunscreen on before I left. It's a forty and lasts all day. Won't sweat off." She finally looked up, out over the hills to the east. Her face took on a pleased expression. She was far away from home now and could relax. I realized that this was one of the few times I had been around Janice when she was not drinking. The wind took liberties with her hair. She stopped for a rest, and Mattie and I stood near her as if she were our charge for the day, needing to protect her and return her home safely. If Mattie and I were about to topple off the edge of the world, Janice was not.

"Can we sit and eat now? I'm tired. My legs are starting to ache." She wasn't embarrassed.

Mattie smiled fondly at her. "Sure, but there's no shade here. Just a little further, five minutes, there's an overhang, we can sit under the rock." She turned and moved up the trail. I waited for Janice to start after her, then I took up the rear.

Yet another odd threesome, I thought, as I watched Janice's vulnerable shape—soft and rounded, a little bent—moving ahead of me. If Pop could have made the hike, we'd have brought him too. A quirky quartet daring the watching rocks not to laugh. All of a sudden I wanted to be alone with Mattie, looking down on Bisbee and the cracked top of the Copper Queen Mine. I wanted Janice to happily be minding the books in the hardware store, and I wanted Pop to be sipping whiskey in the Crystal Palace. A flick of fear made my heart sick. In a moment, it was gone.

Janice's feet brushed precariously close to the cactus as we turned off the trail toward the overhang. Prickly pear and jumping cholla reached out desperately with their spines for her nyloned ankles. She wore baby-blue Keds without socks, her nylons shooting out sparks of light as the sun passed them. Janice lived here—why didn't she think about snakes and cactus? I was slightly annoyed.

"OK. Time to eat." Mattie sat between Janice and me and unpacked lunch. Apples, Hershey Bars, raisins, peanuts, cheese sandwiches. And three lukewarm cans of Coke. She was a happy girl, leaning back on the cool red rock, chewing big bites of sandwich. As I watched her, my chest opened to a smoothness, a calm. After her sandwich was gone, she cut up an apple with her pocket knife and handed us each a slice. Her hands were tan, lines of dirt barely visible under her short fingernails, and her turquoise ring winked at the turquoise sky. Her dark eyes took my face and loved it, whispered to it, reassured it.

"Janice." Mattie's voice deepened with seriousness.

"What, hon?" was the sweet, innocent reply.

"Does Billy have a map, a layout of the tunnels in the mine?"

I shot a quick look of disapproval to Mattie for her abrupt beginning to Janice's adventure.

"A map? What do you mean?" Janice looked at Mattie, then at me, curiosity settling in her eyes.

"A map. A blueprint. A diagram. He must have something from when he had the tunnel bolstered for the train. How did he know which tunnels he could use?"

"Well, I guess he does. He had a friend of his who's a mining engineer work with him. Cost him a bundle, and I wasn't too happy about it. He hasn't broke even yet." Janice pouted into the dirt as she drew circles in it with a twig.

Mattie glanced at me with the slightest bit of enjoyment. I was getting anxious.

Janice stopped her dirt doodling and stated matter-of-factly,

"You know, some of those tunnels have water in them."

My breath stopped. "Which ones?" It came flying out.

Janice gave me a surprised look. "I don't know. Now what's all this interest in those tunnels? Take the train tour. We could use the business!"

The apple was gone. Mattie lit a cigarette and blew a signal out from our cave. A sign to her guardian spirit of her whereabouts. And mine. She looked long and seriously at Janice, who was waiting for something from her. We both waited. This was all Mattie's, and she was making it life or death.

"Janice, do you consider yourself a spiritual person at all?" Mattie was direct and unavoidable.

"Well, yes," Janice's voice squirmed. "Of course we go to church. Billy wants me to teach Sunday school, but I can't speak in front of people. Makes me clam up tight." Her eyes darted over to me, searching for help. I just smiled at her while my mind was stuck on the thought of our tunnel under water. But it couldn't be if dust came out of there. If Jack Timmins' ghost really was in the tunnel, it wouldn't be under water. Could a ghost live under water? The stupid, silent question brought me back to the conversation spreading out over the ground under the weight of the overhanging rock.

Mattie continued. "Do you believe that spirits of people speak to us in our dreams?" *Oh boy.* Janice's eyebrows arched, and then came together in confusion. I took my boots and socks off and let my feet breathe in the breezy shade. We'd be here a while.

Janice was cool. "Well, let me think about that one." She looked sideways at Mattie and said, "You all right?"

Mattie moved herself more toward Janice. "I'm fine. It's just that I see something in you and I've got this wild thing going on and I think maybe you can help me out. You want to give it a shot?"

"Give what a shot?"

Mattie leaned into Janice's face and whispered, "An adventure."

Janice's face stopped in its tracks and froze there a few inches from Mattie's. Then she jerked up straight and announced, "Well, why don't you just try me. You might be surprised."

"Uh-huh," Mattie said slowly, as she leaned back against my shoulder. She smiled at Janice for a long minute.

Janice looked at me and asked, "You part of this thing too?"

"Of course."

"What are you two up to? It's got something to do with that old man, doesn't it?" Her newly found intrigue turned on a light in her eyes.

"Sort of." My reply was vague. I wanted Mattie to keep her momentum. She was doing a great job so far.

Janice's attention turned to Mattie, who challenged her to guess. "See if you can guess what we're doing."

"That's not fair." She paused, examining our eager faces. "Give me a light, will you?" As she exhaled her cigarette smoke, she said, "All right. He's Mattie's long-lost father. You thought your daddy was the one who raised you, but it's really the old man. He had you out of wedlock when he was older, made his cousin raise you and pretend you were his. Your real mother was a prostitute who died two days after you were born in the back room of the whorehouse." She took a drag on her cigarette. "That's not all. There were twins. A boy and a girl. Your twin brother died at birth and that old man, your real daddy, took that dead baby and buried it in one of the tunnels in the Copper Queen Mine."

Mattie and I stared at her with our mouths open, dumbfounded. Janice finished off her story with a "There," as she flicked a cigarette ash into the dirt.

"Nice try, Janice. Did you figure that out on your own, or is that the gossip going around town?" Mattie wasn't amused. I was. Janice was offended.

"I guessed that all on my own."

"You know," I interrupted, "you're not that far off. I mean, there is a relationship here with that old man. His name's Pop. He knew Mattie's grandmother, who died a few years ago." The memory of Lizzy faintly with us in the mine slipped into my head.

"Lizzy Springer," Mattie said, as if Janice would respond, "Oh yeah, I knew her." Anyway we were back on track. Mattie began to tell Janice about a dream she'd had two nights ago. A dream I didn't know about. It ignited my spine as it unfolded high up over Bisbee in the rocky arch of shade.

Mattie's eyes glistened as she told us her dream. "You and Lizzy were standing in the desert, just the two of you and miles of sagebrush." Janice seemed amazed that Mattie would dream about her. Mattie continued with her captive audience. "You were standing over a small hole in the ground, about the size of a garbage can lid. You weren't talking. It was twilight, but you were both unusually bright. The hole was bright, too. A little smoke or something was coming up through the hole. Everything was still and quiet. You were looking at the hole, and suddenly a butterfly came up out of the hole through the smoke. It was tattered and slow, and it kind of hung around a few minutes. Then my grandmother held her hand out and the butterfly landed in her palm."

Janice waited a few seconds before she said, "Is that all?" Mattie nodded. I saw a hawk trying to kick off a pestering crow up in the sky. Janice was still disturbed. "Well, what the hell does that mean?" Mattie and I were looking at each other quietly, and that didn't help. Janice escalated. "I've seen butterflies like that. All faded with pieces missing out of their wings. They can barely fly. They're old and broken up, half dead."

I found myself saying, "Janice, butterflies don't get old. They only live a few days. Their life is only a few days long."

Mattie spoke up. "It's not about the butterfly, it's about the hole." She pulled off her boots and lay back on the ground, hands behind her head. We were going to be here all day arguing about this dream. I pulled my knees up to my chest and wrapped my arms around them for comfort. Janice didn't seem to know what to say now, but she was still upset about the elderly butterfly. She stood up and pulled her pants legs down from their tight grip on her thighs, then sat down again. I knew what the dream was about and why it sent fire through my spine, but I couldn't say it.

We all sat in silence for a minute. I became very aware of the bird songs, and of little canyon wrens darting in and out of the rocks around us. Shadows outside of our shade changed with the traveling afternoon. Mattie was playing with her toes; her eyes were thinking hard. Sections of blonde hair shifted with her slight movements. That feeling of twinship grew in my chest as I felt her spirit try to coax the moment into order. I moved toward her and put my hand on the back of her bent neck, my mouth to her ear. If the caress made Janice uncomfortable, I didn't care. "Ride 'em, cowgirl," I whispered, and Mattie smiled, pressing her head into my face.

"Well, what's it got to do with anything?" Janice's abrupt question seemed to be spoken by a giant sky spirit bent over and talking into our cave. Maybe Mattie's smoke signal had worked. I stood out in the sun and stretched my legs, guessing it was about two o'clock.

Mattie and Janice took up the challenge of the dream.

"I guess it can't be about just one thing. So it's probably about the hole and the butterfly." Mattie seemed fairly convinced.

"And me," Janice said quietly, not sure whether to be happy or perturbed about her role in the dream. I stood out in the sun with my back to them, arms crossed, like some sort of guard.

"Well, yeah," Mattie said, "you are part of this. And that's why we need you to help with the map of the tunnels. You need to get that map for us."

Janice looked upset, but before she could speak Mattie launched into the story.

"Pop is not my father, but he is a friend of my family's. He's a little confused—"

Janice interrupted. "I hear he's senile and doesn't even make sense when he talks."

I was in Janice's face in a split second, spinning around from guard duty to confront that dreaded fact, there, under the ancient, hanging rock. Pop couldn't be senile. I hated that word. He couldn't be a complete goner. Because if he was, then so was I.

"Have you ever talked to him? Have you ever had a conversation with him, listened real close to him?"

I would stare her down until she answered me truthfully. She did.

"No. But that's what people say."

I backed off a little. "Who? Turrell? Nice. You listen to him?"

"No! I hate Turrell. Celita talks about Pop sometimes. Says he's a riot." She looked at her feet, sensing that she'd said the wrong thing.

"Celita said Pop was senile?" I was surprised, but reminded myself that she was just a teenager. "Janice, let's pick another word, a nicer word for a nice man. OK?"

Janice nodded up at me. "All right, what word?"

I thought for a minute. "Kooky. That has a nicer feel to it, doesn't it?"

Mattie joined in with a final statement. "*Kooky* is a silly word. Pop is not silly. Pop is very old. He is demented. His memory is just about shot, and he can't completely take care of himself. He's a survivor of a grand time, a wild time, and everyone he knew from that life is dead. And he's confused about all of that. He believes one of his buddies, you may have heard of him—Wyatt Earp—is still alive and is trapped in a tunnel in the Copper Queen Mine." *Thank you, Mattie.*

I felt sensible again.

"Tunnel 3," I found myself saying. Mattie threw me a curious, impatient look, then continued.

"He trusts me to help him find Wyatt Earp. Because he knew my grandmother, because he loved her, he thinks I'm here to help him and he simply won't take no for an answer. He sees me as some part of that life, I think, because I look like my grandmother. Now I feel like I have to do this for him, get him in the mine and then see what happens."

Janice knew what would happen. "Won't he just be more confused? In the middle of the mine, looking at nothing but that dark rock and dirt? What are you going to do when there's no Wyatt Earp standing there?" She looked at me. "Is that your part? You're going to come out of the shadows dressed like Wyatt Earp, tell him not to worry about you, that you're OK and that he should go home and forget about you?"

Mattie and I stared at her until she was uncomfortable. As she squirmed around I said to Mattie, "Why didn't we think of that. It's perfect." She ignored me.

"Janice, let's look at it this way. Maybe we're fulfilling an old man's last wish. His last burning desire. His only passion. I just know I have to do this, and I need some help."

Janice seemed to seriously consider this notion. She turned to me with a genuine question. "How are you involved in this? Did you two know each other before now?"

I answered. "Seems like we did, but I'd never seen Mattie before she landed with Pop at the hotel. I don't know, Janice. I guess I'm just along for the ride. Kind of pulled in this direction, not really knowing why. But I do feel an obligation to help them get into that mine, into that tunnel. I've got a hunch."

She accepted that, knowing there was more, knowing we were wild for each other, inseparable, teeming lovers. No more questions, though, only, "So you've got to get him way in there. The tour won't do."

"The tour won't do." Mattie reminded Janice that Turrell was a monster and that no one could know about this.

"Please don't tell Celita." I didn't want her to quit, thinking I'd lost my mind.

"God, if I tell anyone, they'll think I'm crazy." She considered what she had just said. "So why don't I think you're crazy?" Janice laughed as her eyes moved back and forth between us.

"It's not crazy," Mattie reminded herself.

I added, "It's just one of those things that comes into your life you never could have predicted. Things in life don't always follow the rules we learned, do they? There are different roads to take that you never see until you're on them sometimes. And people put you on those roads. Mattie and Pop put *me* on this one, and maybe Elizabeth Springer put *them* on it first."

Janice seemed mesmerized and said slowly, "And the dream put me on it." She jerked her head up from its gaze into the dirt at her feet and looked at us as if we'd just told her a horrific ghost story at Girl Scout camp. Then she got up quickly, brushing her pants seat off as she went out into the sun. "I don't know about this one, girls," she said loudly to the desert which had risen up high under her Keds. "Wyatt Earp! He's been dead forever. I'll have to sit on it for a while." She searched vacantly past the hills, squinting into the bright sun. "I have to go home now."

We walked slowly down the trail in silence, the sun pushing hard on our shoulders. Had we made a mistake?

Pop didn't return to the mine the way we thought he would, and he wouldn't really tell me why. "We've got to keep out of sight of that driver," was all he said. I agreed with him.

"I'll walk you back to the hotel, Pop. Mattie's taking a nap." So was he, of sorts, sitting at his table in the cafe, his head bobbing with drowsiness. Or boredom.

He stood up, and I touched his arm gently as we made our way to his temporary home. He didn't head for the bar like he usually did. Instead, he went for the stairs to his room.

"Bring me a whiskey." He paused at the foot of the stairs and stared squarely at me. His eyes were watery.

We shared the stare for a good minute. "Want to go to the bar with me?" I said, finally.

"He might be in there. Bring me my whiskey up here."

I walked up with him, asking him who he was talking about. He moved to the deep, stuffed chair by the window in his room, looking like a skinny stamen in a lush red flower as he sank into the chair's plushness. He wouldn't answer.

"I'll be back in a minute," I said, shutting the door a little too hard. Now what was this new caving in? What would we do if Pop slipped away into his crumbling mind? Too many turns in this road, I thought as I walked into the bar. When I ordered him a shot, Alice the bartender asked me if I'd seen Janice Beecham. Something made me say, "No."

"Her husband called here about ten minutes ago looking for her." Alice appeared less interested in Janice's whereabouts than I'm sure she was.

"Can't help you," I lied as I walked off with the shot glass. What would Alice do anyway if she knew I'd left Janice at her car only twenty minutes ago? Call Billy? It was none of his business—or Alice's. Besides, Billy Beecham was more of an enemy than ever now: he had something we wanted. I pictured Janice looking through Billy's desk drawers while he was out of the house, looking for the magic tunnel map. My picture was more like a menacing scene from a silent movie than reality.

Pop opened his door slowly after my second knock. He reached his hand through the narrow opening and took his whiskey without a word. Then he shut the door. An emptiness, a sadness filled the hallway where I stood, and I was lost. I had forgotten my lines.

My key clicked softly in Mattie's door. I peeked in the room as the door swung open with a quiet creak. She wasn't asleep.

"Hey," I said gently, "did you sleep?"

"For a few minutes." She held her arms out for me from the bed, and the void of the hallway slipped away.

I lay down next to her and kissed each closed eyelid. I stared up at the lightless, flat glass globe on the ceiling, feeling robbed of a new star in the galaxy. A fake. A false front for an old light bulb holding on tight to its secrets. I turned to Mattie and sighed.

"Pop is afraid of Turrell now."

Mattie sat up, surprised. "Afraid? How do you know?"

"He told me that we have to keep away from him, keep out of his sight." I sat up, too, and smiled broadly as a delightful image came to me. "We'll have Pop call Turrell out of Elmo's tomorrow. Pop will be waiting for him in the street with both six-guns ready to jump from his holsters. Just in case Pop's not fast enough, I'll be up on the roof across the street with a shotgun pointed right at Turrell."

"Great idea." Mattie wasn't that impressed. "He's afraid of him. So that's why he's not going back to the mine."

"I guess so."

"I wonder if he should be afraid of him."

"I don't know. Maybe. But Celita keeps her eye on him when he's in the cafe. So does Baby. Turrell won't dare show his face in there anymore."

"Why?"

"He just won't." I looked convincingly at Mattie. "Celita is to call the sheriff if he so much as puts his hand on the door."

"Let's take Pop over the border for some good dinner."

Mattie got out of bed and stood looking at me. I saw in her eyes the dark comfort of trust that comes home to a child asleep at night amid the sounds of crickets and frogs.

"And some good music," I added. "I haven't taken you to La Caverna yet." Her eyes and the thought of the turquoise tiled bar, the rock walls, and the sweaty white-shirted mariachi band broke through all concern about the menacing Turrell. "We'll buy Pop a big cigar."

We grabbed him from his slow whiskey, and the jeep took off down the road with the radio blaring and the wind slapping everyone. Mattie and I laughed as we sang along loudly with Tammy Wynette's "Stand By Your Man." I saw Pop's face light up in the rearview mirror with the passing cars' headlights. Each shining pass painted the same picture: he was smiling. The twilight whisked us across the border.

"Here you go mister, just for you." I handed him the long green cigar with a big grin on my face. Pop looked around the noisy bar before he took it. Mattie lit it for him, and he settled happily into his first cloud of sweet smoke, his small darting eyes barely visible.

Mattie and I held hands under the table as the mariachis sang to us. She was trying, over the music and stir of the crowd, to tell me about a trip to the Yucatan that she took with Lizzy. I listened to everything at once, so my impression of their trip gained color, background music, and a cast of thousands. The cloud of smoke cleared over Pop's head. Then the world seemed to tilt as I recognized Janice coming through the door, her red lofty hair and bare shoulders floating just above the heads of people seated at tables.

Janice had a cigarette hanging out of her mouth, a drink in one hand, and her purse in the other. She and Billy and another couple made their way into the bar from the restaurant—past the crowd at the bar, past the mariachi band, right smack in front of our table. I stared at her while Mattie talked on, unaware of Janice standing two feet away.

Janice's drunken, slow-motion eyes bobbed like ghosts through the crowd, finally landing on us. She hollered, "Mattie! Kate!" She was loaded. Mattie looked up and froze. We hadn't been sure about Janice since our disclosure about Pop and Wyatt Earp. And I didn't trust her mouth when she was drunk. Oblivious to the impending deluge of Janice, Pop blew another thick cloud into the scene. Janice plopped down next to him and waved Billy and the others on from their curious pause. Billy's mouth was so tight he looked like he had only one thin lip. He led the couple to a table.

Janice's head swam from Pop to us and back to Pop. She was delighted. "What the hell are you doing here?"

Mattie spoke first. My tight throat kept all future words hostage. "Having a few drinks. You?" Her slight coldness didn't faze Janice, whose attention was on Pop.

"You must be Pop!" She tried to focus on him through the smoke, finally sticking her face into the cloud. "I've been dyin' to meet you, mister," she said loudly as she fumbled with a pack of cigarettes. "I hear you're a wild kinda guy, and I believe it, cavorting around with these two gals!" Her face pulled out of the smoky cloud and she took a gulp of her drink. "Let me buy some drinks here. You're all so cute." She looked at our glasses. "What are you drinking?"

I smiled and forced out my first words, "We're OK, thanks."

"Well, good for you. Pop, come on, you want another drink don't you? And what's the gentleman having?" The music had stopped, but she was still talking loudly, hushing the crowd a little. In her hand a cigarette flapped wildly over the table. She jabbed Pop with her elbow, snickering at some foiled joke she'd told him. Pop was not looking at Janice; his eyes were trained on the end of his cigar as if on a rifle's sight. She clumsily motioned for the waiter and ordered the drinks. I stole a glance over to Billy's table.

"Janice, Billy's looking like he wants you to get over there," I lied.

"Oh, shit. Well, isn't that just too bad. Light my cigarette, Pop, will you?"

Mattie lit it for her. "Janice, why don't we talk some other time, OK?"

Janice looked at each of us. The drinks came. She raised her glass and said, "OK, honey. First, one little toast. To the Copper

Queen!" We stopped breathing. Leaning over the table close to our faces, she began a long grin, then said slowly and quietly, "I found it." She pushed herself back from the table, got up, and took her grin away into the crowd. Mattie and I stared into the empty space across from us, turned to each other, stunned, then looked back to the space where Janice had been. In her place was a fresh, thick cloud of smoke.

14

"Maybe we should all move in together in my house. Never mind, I didn't say that." I teased Mattie's look of amazement. "Well, I could ask Pop. He never gets any say in anything here. I'm sure he'd love it, but," I spoke to Mattie's look, "it's not as convenient as the hotel. You're right."

"Kate—"

"Don't you fret, baby, I'm just teasing you." I kissed her mouth as it tried to talk and failed. "Now, I want to hear about this butterfly dream again. Why didn't you tell me? You need to tell me these things. We saw Lizzy in the mine. She left us her hat. You've got to tell me."

She refilled her coffee cup and sat down next to me on my couch. The sun was tiptoeing in, disguised as yellow squares on the floor. Her voice was a little shaky when she said, "It's not just about the butterfly. I don't know why I couldn't tell you. I was going to, a few times, and I couldn't get it out." I remembered the mule I felt that day in the mine and that I hadn't been able to tell Mattie about it.

"Matt, I know it's about the hole and the butterfly. But you know what? The butterfly is transformation. It's us." My eyes squinted at the traveling yellow squares on the floor. "I just don't know why Janice was there."

Before she looked away, as she started to cry, I caught a glimpse of helpless love on her face. I put my arm around her and couldn't think of a single thing to say. Then I told her about the mule in the mine. About thinking I was with the mule and hearing the sounds of miners before we saw Lizzy. And that somehow the words wouldn't come to tell her. She stopped crying, wiping her wet eyes with the palms of her hands.

We sat there for a while. The room had become bright and clear, the yellow squares spreading over the floor, crawling up our legs. Mattie turned her forehead against my cheek. I let my fingers wander through her hair and I thought of all the times she had cried.

"We'd better get going. Pop's probably finished his coffee." Mattie sighed as her hands pushed off from her sunlit legs. She rose from the couch, the last constellation in my morning sky. We weren't going to talk about the dream or the mule or Lizzy, and I didn't know why.

Noisy cicadas walked us down the road. We stopped abruptly when we saw Pop struggling toward us, Turrell beside him. Pop was jerking his arm away as Turrell poked it with a finger. I don't know what he was saying, but Pop wasn't happy. A blaze ran up my spine—I don't even know if Mattie saw the two of them before I bolted. I was in front of them in a second.

Standing between them, I faced Turrell with an imaginary shotgun in my voice. "What are you doing?"

"None of your business. Get outta my way." He tried to walk around me, but I moved to block him. Mattie came up and stood between me and Turrell and Pop.

"I think it *is* my business. You're bothering my friend and I want you to turn your ugly ass around and get—"

"Fuck your—"

My voice jumped loudly in his face. "Pop does not want to talk to you. Get off my street!" I was going to explode, and there would be fragments in the road—from all of us—to show for it.

Turrell was drunk. "Your street? Well, aren't you just little miss shit!" He was laughing as he stumbled away.

The three of us stood there until he disappeared and we couldn't hear his scraping boot heels. Then I took Pop by the arm. "Come on. Let's go back to the cafe." I burst into the cafe ahead of Pop and Mattie, ignoring several customers, and was behind the counter in no time. Celita looked at me with apprehension as she stopped what she was doing.

"Did Turrell come in here?" I demanded. "Did he come in here?"

"He came in and was talking to Pop. He didn't—"

"I told you to call the sheriff, Celita, if he ever came in here again."

"He didn't do anything. I didn't know if I should call the sheriff: you weren't here, and I wasn't sure!"

Her eyes teared, her upper lip quivered. Steam from the stove circled around our faces. Suddenly I felt my own tears. My rage slid down my body, landing softly on the floor, and I put my hand on her shoulder.

"Honey, I'm sorry. I shouldn't put you in a position like that. I'm sorry. I didn't mean to do that to you. It's OK. I'll take care of it."

Her face relaxed. "Now, did he take Pop out of here? What happened?"

"Pop got up and left and Turrell went out behind him. I don't know what happened after that. What's wrong?"

"It's OK, we can talk about it later. I'm sorry. It's not that big a deal." I walked through the staring customers over to the table where Pop and Mattie had settled. Mattie's eyes were as black as the mine and they gripped my shirt and pulled me to her. I sat down with no words.

She explored my eyes. "Kate?" she whispered. I was crying. She squeezed my hand with one hand and leaned her forehead into the other one. Wiping my eyes with a dirty, crumpled napkin, I caught Pop looking at me. His eyes were big and bright and moist. His lips were moving in silence. I had dipped into the well of his fright when I saw Pop trying to get to my house, and now we sank together, to the bottom.

Celita wiped her hands on her damp apron and pulled a can of Coke from the cooler. She walked over to my table and sat down across from me. I looked at her, waiting. The cafe settled into its emptiness like a spinning nickel slowing to a stop on the floor. Outside, the town pulsed quietly, slowly, into the end of the day. By now Mattie and Pop would be in the Turquoise Bar in Gleeson, sipping drinks and listening to old Swede play his drunken fiddle.

My favorite ghost town, Gleeson, sported chimneys poking from ruins and one standing building, the Turquoise Bar. Swede would show them the bullet hole in the post that had held the ceiling up for a hundred years and tell them one of a variety of stories of how the bullet hole got there. I was wishing I'd gone with them, if for nothing else than to look into the long glass case full of dusty chunks of turquoise and forget about Turrell and today's eruption. But what I really wanted was one simple thing: to sit alone in my empty cafe and wait for dusk to seep in through the screen door. My long-standing annoyance at Turrell had turned into rage, and it didn't feel like mine, like this would happen to me, here. If I could just be alone, maybe I could get a grip on it. But here was Celita, looking suddenly grown up, staring at me with a serious face.

"Why didn't Francisco come down today?" I asked, noticing the few decaying spots of red relic on her fingernails.

"Said he didn't feel like it. He gets that way once in a while. What are you going to do." It wasn't a question.

"Sit here, hopefully alone, for a few hours."

"I mean with your life, the cafe," she challenged.

I spit out a sneery laugh and looked around the tired room. "Sell it. Want to buy it?"

"I'm seventeen!" She was appalled at my irrational answer.

I sunk further into my chair and sighed. "I know you're seventeen, Celita. I wasn't being serious."

She leaned toward me on her elbows, gripping the sweating can of Coke with both hands. "You know, I've been pretty quiet all along. I haven't said much."

I was cornered. "About what?"

"Mattie and Pop. And you. And you and Mattie. And suddenly Janice is your best friend."

"Now wait a minute. You know that Janice is not my best friend." I didn't really want to have this conversation. "Mattie and me we can talk about, but not Janice. She's as much my best friend as she is yours."

She switched channels. "It's incredible that you and Mattie were born on the same day. I've never met anyone born on my birthday. You're astral twins."

I squinted my eyes at her. "What's an astral twin?"

She frowned. "I don't know. But that's what people are saying."

"Who?"

"Thea. And Carla. John Belton says you will always fly together. He wants to do your reading or something. And a couple old ladies said you are soul mates."

My eyes told her the truth. "We're lovers."

"They said that, too."

"Well, isn't that nice. Any questions I have about my life, I know who to go to."

"Thea brought a weird clock in and made me put it on top of the cash register. She said you bought it and told me to give her thirty-five dollars."

"It's OK. I'll reimburse the till. I asked her to get it for me. How do you like it?" I looked across the room at the thing perched proudly on its new home. "I think it looks great." Celita knew that this was the first time I'd seen it.

"You haven't noticed it? It's been there all week!"

"Sorry—"

"I don't like it."

"It stays." I looked hard at her angry, pouting face. "What's wrong, Celita?"

"I know you don't care about the cafe anymore."

I was surprised that the lack of my presence would bother Celita so much. "Well, what does that mean? Are you having trouble? Is it too much work for you?"

"No, that's OK. It's just, you know." She busied her mouth with a big gulp of Coke.

"No, I don't know." I pulled myself back up straight in my chair. "What's on your mind, sweetie?"

Words suddenly spewed out of her mouth like water out of a broken fire hydrant. "I want to know what's going on with Pop. And Mattie. Everyone's talking about it, and I don't know what to say to them!"

I raised my hand between us. "Excuse me, why do you have to say anything to them?" Who *they* were didn't matter. *They* were everyone on the planet. Suddenly I could feel Celita's attachment, her grip on the shirttails of my life. I thought she was going to cry. Everyone was crying now. Everyone. What the hell was going on?

She fought the tears. "So, so they'll know you're, you're not..." She couldn't finish.

"So they'll know I'm not crazy? A lunatic? A werewolf? Dracula? A spy?"

She looked down. I added my hands to hers around the Coke can. "Look, honey, you don't have to protect me, I can do that OK. I'm sorry if this has been rough on you." As I focused on the top of her head, my eyes expanded, and the tired, dimming room snapped into a crisp world of shining tabletops and glowing stone walls. Celita's face lifted up, bright and wondering. "What do you want to know?" I asked.

"Why is Pop here with Mattie?" She relaxed.

"He wanted her to bring him here." I paused. "He wants to look in the mine for something, and she's going to help him."

"For what?"

"I'm not sure." Well, I wasn't really sure.

"Who's Elizabeth?"

"What?" That one got me. "Why—"

"He keeps talking about Elizabeth. It's kind of confusing. Something about a horse. Something about waiting for her."

"What does he say, what else?"

"I don't know, he talks to Baby. She tells me. She thinks it's funny. She'll sit with him, and I have to yell at her to get to work."

She gave me a look of regret at letting out that bit of information. "I think that's why my grandfather won't come as much, because Baby horns in. If she sees you coming, she jumps up so you won't know. He just keeps talking. But you know, people don't mess with him. Sometimes they stare at him, but most everybody's used to him now. Every time you and Mattie are in here, everyone starts buzzing after you leave. The most popular story is that Pop has some money from a bank robbery buried in the mine." She looked at me out of the corner of her eyes, hoping I'd spill the beans. "Is that true?"

"I don't know. No. Who knows?" I pushed my chair back from the table and paced around the room. "Celita." I stopped at her chair and crossed my arms. "No one knows why Pop wants to go in that mine. He doesn't really know either because he's so confused. He's got everything all mixed up from his life. Elizabeth is Mattie's grandmother. He knew her. Mattie looks a lot like Elizabeth, and I think he's mixing them up. He supposedly used to ride with Wyatt Earp—" I stopped. "Do you know who Wyatt Earp is?"

She rolled her eyes. "Yes, I know who Wyatt Earp is."

"OK. He's even got him mixed up in this. All I know is that we are going to help him out."

"With what?" It was an innocent question that stopped me cold. I sat down and said flatly, "I'm going to get them in the mine."

Celita looked at me, confused. "Kate, he took the train tour. He's been in the mine. I don't understand this." She finished the Coke and sat back in her chair.

"Me neither. Well, see, I think he should go back in the other tunnels, not just where the train goes. One in particular. It's a hunch."

"A hunch?" I wasn't helping.

"Yeah. The tunnel with the ghost in it. I think somehow it'll take care of this whole thing for Pop."

She got up and took her apron off. "It sure will! It'll scare him to death. That's cruel."

She believed the ghost story! I walked after her, surprised. "Cruel?"

She headed for the door, tossing her apron on the counter on her way. "This is a very weird thing. I gotta go." Halfway out the door she turned and said to me, annoyed, "I won't tell anyone."

I stood in the middle of the embarrassed cafe, staring at the screen door, wondering what had just happened. And where was the dusk, anyway?

I stared straight ahead, dreaming, waiting on the floor of the dark cafe. Waiting for Mattie to get back. Waiting for Janice to emerge out of the dark earth holding a dirty map in her hand. Waiting for Celita to put a wet washcloth on my feverish forehead. Waiting for the lights to come on all by themselves. Bad bulbs. Dusk mania. I had hypnotized myself until the screen door exploded and Mattie walked in.

"What are you doing? Can I turn on a light?"

"Just one little one, please." My legs were stiff from sitting in one position for so long.

The dim glow from the lamp on the counter stretched across the room as far as it could. "Hi," I said, as I stood up awkwardly.

Mattie sat at the counter with her eyes on me and lit a cigarette. "I really think I should have left Pop in the Turquoise Bar to live out the rest of his life with Swede. I think that would have been the best thing to do. I should have done it."

I tiptoed through the sleeping tables toward her. "Maybe. Let's get out of here." We walked out onto the lonely street.

"Did you get your respite? Feel better?" She ran a finger down my spine, electrifying it, aiming straight up into the endless sky like an arrow.

"No."

"No? What happened?"

"Celita's being needy. She says everyone thinks Pop has some stolen money buried in the mine. He's here with you to get it. And I'm from Pluto. Do you know that Pop talks to Baby about Elizabeth? Sort of. Anyway, Celita's thinking I'm out of my mind. But she won't tell anybody."

I looked up at the stars. I thought I saw Pluto calling me back home. We began to walk slowly down the street.

"What did he say about Elizabeth?" Mattie took my hand.

"I don't know. We'll have to ask Baby, I guess. Sounds like she's running Francisco off, horning in on Pop. I wonder why she's so taken with Pop. You haven't seen Janice, have you?"

"No. I guess she'll get in touch with us somehow. Maybe she was lying, teasing us when she said she found it."

"No, I think she found it. Maybe she doesn't actually have it yet." We sat on the porch of the hotel. No one was around. "Wonder why it's so deserted here tonight."

Mattie sighed. "I feel like Long John Silver trying to get that treasure map."

"You are. We both are. Two looney pirates sneaking around in the dark with big knives between our teeth."

"You're tired. Come on, let's go to your house and see what's on TV."

I knew I would fall asleep. Halfway through a "Gunsmoke" rerun, Miss Kitty smiled and wooed me to Dodge City. In the morning, my eyes popped open to pounding on my front door. Where was Mattie? The pounding was relentless. I got up against my will, and the thought that something had happened to Pop shot through my veins. I threw on a shirt and shorts and flew to the door. No one was there when I opened it. The pounding continued.

I looked on the porch and there was Mattie stretching her beautiful limbs up the wall, hammering a long nail into the wood of my house. She had a satisfied smile on her face as she stepped back to admire her handiwork, shoving the hammer through a belt loop on her jeans. Without a word, I went over to see what she was doing. My sleepy eyes fell on two huge horseshoes hanging on two big nails. They were heavy steel with a thin coat of rust, and very worn. Mattie stood with her hands on her hips, waiting for me to say something. I looked closer. I touched them. They were hot.

She couldn't wait any longer. "I left them in the jeep last night, wanted you to see them in the sunlight. We found them yesterday in

Gleeson, out near an abandoned mine." Her eyes sparkled. "They are, without a doubt, the biggest shoes I've ever seen. They go with your necklace—a matching set!"

She lifted one of them off the nail and laid it into my hands. "It's heavy. Don't drop it."

I put it to my nose first. It smelled like a handful of old pennies. As I turned it over, its heat hummed in my hands. I felt the warmth crawl up my arms. The top of my head began to tingle. When Mattie took it from me, I couldn't move my hands back to their normal happy-go-lucky mode. I just stood there, silent, with warm arms. Mattie really wanted me to tell her how incredible they were. All I could say was, "They're astral twins."

Mattie scowled and led me back into the house. She sat me down at the kitchen table and turned on the burner under the tea kettle. Kneeling beside me and taking my hand, she said impatiently, "What's going on, Kate?"

Two large tears squirted from my eyes, one for each horseshoe. "Nothing. Mattie, they're so wonderful. I love them. I love you. Did you know we're astral twins?" The tea kettle was working up a soft whistle. Mattie kissed me until it began to howl and blow steam like a train bound for glory.

15

We spent more time with Pop at his table in the cafe, hoping he might let us in on his secrets, but he wouldn't talk very much when we were there. We would have to leave him to Baby and then wring information out of her. The horseshoe clock did look great on the cash register, and it took on new meaning for me now that the largest horseshoes in the world were hanging on my house. The hot steel of those two mammoths glowed in my eyes. They were always with me, but I couldn't talk about them. I spent as much time as possible sitting on the porch, staring at them. I think I was waiting for them to speak to me.

Pop ignored us across the table, shooting us with his go-away-six-gun.

"Well, why don't we leave Pop to his friends and mosey on along?"

"Sure," Mattie said, standing up. "Pop, you want to go back to Gleeson sometime?" He shook his head from side to side and mumbled. She looked at me, confused, wondering at Pop's change of heart about Gleeson. He had loved it. He had seemed elated there, laughing at Swede and his stories, drinking whiskey by a bullet hole. He crept around the ruins of houses and aborted mining operations. He bent over and picked up old rusty tin cans, turned them over in his hands, and then put them back down in the desert. He found the horseshoes. He stood pointing down at them until Mattie came over and claimed them. He kept looking in the back seat at his find on the ride back to Bisbee. But he never said anything about them.

We were getting ready to leave when Celita came over holding something in a plastic bag. "I was babysitting at the Beechams' last night, and Janice asked me to give you this." Of course she had a little suspicious gleam in her eye. I took the bag in my hand. "Thanks. I think the clock looks great. You'll learn to like it." I headed straight for the door with Mattie right behind me. We made a beeline for the hotel and ran up the stairs to her room.

"Hey, girls! Don't speak!" Carla's voice ran up the stairs behind us.

Inside the K-Mart plastic shopping bag was an old book. A book of poetry by someone I'd never heard of. It was a library book, overdue by about twenty years. A folded paper reached out from its pages. We sat on the bed with the book between us, unwilling to slide that paper out into our hands, out into the light. We watched the unmoving book for what seemed like hours.

"She must've looked for this right after we talked to her about it. I can't believe it. I wasn't really sure she'd do it." I was stunned. Janice. Janice was going to get us in our tunnel. I couldn't help but expect that some other odd turn of events lurked in the shadows.

Mattie stared at the book. "This means we're going to do it. This means we are taking Pop into the mine, back into the tunnels, to look for Wyatt Earp. God..." She picked up the book and opened it to the place where the paper was. She took it out. The book was so worn that it stayed open when she put it back down on the bed, the two pages spread wide apart. "You look at it." She shoved the paper toward me.

I could hear my life screeching to a halt in the distance as I opened the paper. There were only a few words on it—no map, no tunnels. Just Janice saying that she was sorry, but she just couldn't steal from her husband. We could keep the book. Mattie must have recognized the bitter disappointment on my face and leaned forward over the note, reading it upside down. "She can't do it," she said, annoyed, getting up to light a cigarette. "Shit."

Desperation sank in her chest as Mattie hung her head in the blue smoke. She said flatly, "We better take the train tour. Maybe we can somehow find out where that tunnel is."

"I can't ride on that stupid train with Turrell. I can't." I could not solicit information from the most hideous asshole in Bisbee. In

Arizona.

"Well, I can. I can go again with Pop."

"Pop won't go. He's afraid of Turrell, remember?"

"Well, I can't go by myself!" Mattie was ready for a good fight. I wasn't. "Look. Let's take some time with this. I don't want Turrell to have the slightest clue from us about any of it. Besides, you already took the tour and got no clues about that tunnel. We need to think."

I left the bed for the escape hatch of the window. Carla was taking a break in the street with John Belton, the hotel cook, probably giving him the latest update on the astral twins. *What was the latest update?* Janice's note lay on the bed, dying. I turned to Mattie. "I'm going to find someone to go in the mine with us who knows where that tunnel is. But right now, I'm going to talk to John Belton." I put the note back in the waiting book, kissed my beautiful compadre, and walked heavily down the darkening afternoon stairs.

I ran into Carla and John as they came through the hotel door in their usual fashion—John scurrying in Carla's wake, in his romantic pursuit of her old ambivalence.

"Hey, John. Carla. How's it going?"

They smiled, acknowledging that business was slowing down, probably the heat. Same as last summer. It would pick up in the fall.

"Uh, John, can I talk to you for a minute?" My eyes asked Carla to please leave, and John and I moved awkwardly toward the other side of the lobby. The secretiveness was a waste. I knew John would tell Carla. It was my little dramatic gift to them.

"John, you do some kind of readings, psychic readings?"

He smiled and nodded.

"Will you do a reading for me?" I stared at my boots.

The dimly lit corner of the lobby was the perfect place for an under-the-breath conversation. He loved it. He sat me on the couch next to him. "I'll do it for free." John's eyes were too close together, and he hardly had any eyebrows. I couldn't look him square in the face. But now I made myself. He seemed about fifty, although he had a fuzzy pubescent beard adorning his chin. It was light colored, like his long, thin hair. And there were his eyes. I forced myself to stick with them, and I began to feel their sharpness, their odd, blue trustworthiness. They had no choices in life, and they stood their ground. Tough little guys. Dancing just a little with John's serious excitement.

"I'll do both of you if you want. It's up to you, but I think it's a good idea. When?"

"Give me your number and I'll call you." We went to the desk. Carla gave John a pen and a piece of paper. She treated our exchange with great respect and protection, coming down on the light side of her ambivalence. John's lanky frame moved away to the kitchen, and I left with his phone number sizzling in my hip pocket.

Crickets lured Mattie and me into my bed under a half moon. The warm sheet rested lightly on our skin. The lamplight fell graciously onto Janice's old library book. I turned to the pages that had held the note, the note Mattie had burned in the ashtray, wishing on Janice nightmares about her brain being on fire. "Here. Let me read a poem to you. A poem sent on the wings of Janice's chicken Keds, from an inscription on the tomb of the Unknown Hippie Poet." I smiled. Mattie closed her eyes and lay her head back.

As I began to read the strange little poem, my spine heated up and the top of my head became light, then disappeared.

> Mule in the Moon
>
> escaped from the dark distance
> of a lonely moon
> beaten by blindness,
> the mule leaps down
> through the dances of planets,
> shattering the starry gatherings
> with its silver shoes and
> landing on its lightless ribs
> in a caress of treetops
> who sway and whisper
> its fallen song.

Mattie's eyes were open. Frozen. I stared at the poem, suddenly feeling very anxious. The top of my head returned. I got up, still holding the book, and walked to the door, then back to the bed again. "I'm never going to sleep tonight."

Mattie took the book from me, threw it on the floor, and pulled me into bed. She wrapped herself around me. I tucked myself in tight, and we didn't budge. Outside, unseen but felt, the moon was swelling, upsetting the coyotes, upsetting everyone.

16

Baby flung herself into the chair across from us. She looked down at her lap and untied her apron, only to tie it again in nervousness. Celita flipped the *Closed* sign around in the window to face the sidewalk and then disappeared behind the counter to clean up the day's work. The grand inquisition had begun.

"You know Pop is my responsibility," Mattie said with a low, pushing voice. "Anything going on with him, I should know about."

Baby rolled her eyes up from their downward stare without moving her head. "Where did he go?" she mumbled.

"He's at the hotel bar. Now, I need to know if his confusion, or his memory loss, is getting worse. Sometimes he talks enough to me so I can keep a grip on it. Or he talks to Kate. But if he talks a lot to you, I need to know. OK?"

"Yeah, that's OK." She was shaking her leg under the table and the tabletop shimmied.

Mattie watched Baby's face for a minute. The grip of the silence, and the dancing salt-and-pepper shakers, tightened around my spine until I blurted out, "Pop's a pretty neat guy, isn't he?"

Baby ended her slouch and shimmy and said, "He knows a lot. About love and stuff. And he knows he can never go back to Tombstone." She waited for us to be impressed. Then she began having trouble knowing just what to do with her hands.

Mattie smiled. "He knows a lot. About a lot of things. Not all of which I understand, though. Maybe you can help me."

Baby's eyebrows rose and her lids closed for a few seconds before she spoke to Mattie. Her hands continued their futile search for a thing to call home. "He told me all about hiding out in Mexico and about his love affair and his gunfights. OK?"

Mattie sat up straight as a board. "He told you those things, clearly, and in detail?"

"Hiding out in Mexico?" I wanted every mumbly detail.

Mattie waved a hand in the air. "Wait a minute. Baby, did he explain things in detail? You could understand him?"

Her hands found her hair. "Well, sort of. You kind of have to fill in the blanks."

Mattie relaxed into her chair. Clanging pots and forks and glasses reminded us that Celita was there. We were keeping Baby from her job helping Celita clean up. I became aware of how hard Celita worked, of how hopelessly attached to this cafe she was. And of how much I had been not there for whatever she might need. Francisco came less and less—how was she getting him to eat? I gave up on the interrogation of Baby and went to help Celita scrub and wash and sweat.

My absence didn't seem to affect Baby's stories, and Mattie was quite pleased with the results. Late that afternoon, we waited for dusk at the pit, watching the sun set its deathly depths on fire all the way down to the poison pools reflecting the red sky. Our skin glowed and drank the hot, deep color until it faded to gray, giving way to jumping stars hurrying to be first in the night. The breeze was still a little warm.

I imagined Pop sitting in the bar at the hotel, wide awake, waiting for us, or something, and never quite figuring out why. But just waiting. Maybe for Elizabeth to knock softly at his door in the middle of the night. Or for his enemy to make a move for his gun in the hot sun of western insanity. For Wyatt to contact him. For the right soft word from Francisco. Or for Turrell to kick down his door. I could see him sitting at the bar, staring through all those possibilities. I looked toward the hotel. Electric lights now defined the town—the house tops, the front doors—as the night stole their shapes and crept away. The wind brought the faint call of the train pushing through Benson, fifty miles to the north. That struck me as odd.

"How can we hear that train fifty miles away?"

Mattie knew. "Sometimes in the fall, when the wind is just right, in Tucson, I can smell the ocean. From the Sea of Cortez. And that's over two hundred miles away."

I tried to conjure up the smell of dying stranded crabs in the sand, of flattening jellyfish at the water's edge. Of seaweed and salt. I heard shrieking kids and thudding waves. Seagulls crying. I remembered the joy of my eight-year-old self, constructing forts and moats from heavy wet sand, sunburn, the taste of salt in my mouth, and my mother always, always watching from a short distance. I thought of how long it had been since I had been to the ocean. But here was an ocean in front of me, and all around me. Minus the water, it smelled hard, metallic, and of desert sage.

"Baby somehow thinks that knowing Pop Walker will separate her from the rest of her friends, from the rest of her life. That now her life is completely different in a way that means she doesn't have to go to school, or listen to her parents, or take a bath. It means she can drink beer. It means she is really thirty. I told her to think of him as a black-and-white glossy of a famous deceased movie star. A photograph on her bedroom wall, autographed in 1960. A special possession she could treasure when she was doing her homework or making her bed." Mattie was annoyed, but amusing herself. "He's been telling her all kinds of things."

I came back from the beach. "Sensible things?"

"I guess." A lone, high lamplight found our heads from a fence pole. Mattie's eyes were across from me, black, reaching. "He keeps talking about someone named Blue. Another gunfighter, maybe."

"A mule, maybe."

She thought about that one. "Maybe. You and your mule." She said it with affection. "But Blue sounds more like a man the way he refers to him. And Elizabeth, he talks about her angrily sometimes. Like she did something he didn't like, and he says that she's late."

I looked to the south. "You know these mountains are called the Mule Mountains." That brought on a little silence, a little reverence.

Mattie continued. "Baby said he talks mostly about Elizabeth, and it's like he's actually talking to her. He talks about the mine, about Wyatt, about some horse. About someplace in Mexico where no one will find him. And some other person—Baby can't figure out who. She just listens. She doesn't try to put any of it together or question it because it's so disjointed. Sometimes she responds with a 'that's incredible.' She has no clue that this is a real thing."

I had to laugh. *A real thing.* This was not a puzzle with Pop holding the pieces. This was a life in pain, lost, with very few landmarks left. Mattie ignored me. "She said one wonderful thing." I stopped laughing and waited. "She said one day he stood up and announced to everyone in the cafe that he was leaving now, and he was taking Elizabeth with him, and if any of them tried to stop him, he would shoot them. He looked at Baby and told her to get his horse. Then he handed her a piece of paper from his pocket and told her to give it to Wyatt. He stood watching everyone eating and chatting, ignoring his display, and gradually he became confused and sat down." She pulled a piece of paper from her pocket and handed it to me. It was Pop's note to Wyatt. I read it out loud. *"I soon found Elizabeth the mine is too dark time. Yellow for Elizabeth's hands."*

I looked up from the paper, a little stunned. "What the hell is this supposed to mean?"

Mattie shrugged her shoulders in the overhead streetlamp's narrow beam. "His grammar's pretty bad. Well, I guess it's his brain that's pretty bad. But think of it, Kate, he's writing things."

A picture of Pop sitting in his room slid into my mind. He was writing notes, trying to communicate with the ghosts, the tumbleweeds blowing too fast through his head. He was trying to talk to someone.

What did he do with his notes? "Maybe he has other notes like this in his room or in his pockets. Maybe he's been passing them out all over town."

"Let's look in his room."

When we left Pop in the cafe the next morning, I was aware that we were overly nice to him. Celita glared at us over the counter. It was really hard to get away with anything in this town. About the only secret Mattie and I had left was our magic key to the mine.

His room needed airing out. I pushed up the windows as far as their old crooked frame would let me. Mattie started looking through the drawers, through his small vinyl suitcase.

"You think you're going to find a note with directions to the tunnel," I teased. Then I suddenly had a thought. "I bet he's been in that mine before. I bet he has."

"I don't see anything." Mattie sat down on his bed and took out a cigarette.

"Don't light that, he'll know we were here," I said guiltily. She nodded and put the cigarette away. "Carla will probably tell him anyway."

"She said she wouldn't." I believed Carla. She would want us to be successful at whatever it was we were doing. She would not ruin any drama offered during her watch. Carla often had just the missing ingredient to a dilemma and worked hard to find it, in case she was ever asked.

A dog was barking outside and wouldn't stop. I looked out the window to see Turrell sidestepping the annoyed, hot, skinny mutt. I wanted to yell *Kill* out the window, but impatient white fangs fended off Turrell's dying-to-kick boots, and the most miserable man in Bisbee quickly disappeared. Satisfied, and wagging its tail, the lonely, four-legged cowpoke trotted down the street and around the corner out of sight. "It was Turrell. That dog was barking at Turrell."

"Like you—barking at Turrell," Mattie said as she came over to the window to look.

I snickered. "Got him off of the street."

She turned back to her work. "Then the streets are safe. Where would he keep his notes?"

"If they even exist. I don't know. Maybe he—wait a minute. Wait a minute." I knew. I pulled up the mattress. A little stack of papers about an inch thick bound together with a rubberband shielded their eyes from the light. I held them up to Mattie and said, "It was either there or in his hat."

We walked up the canyon with the wad of notes stuffed in my pants pocket. Up past singing cicadas in the mesquite trees, up past the nosy gray boulder pushing against the curve in the road, up to my perched house near the canyon's end. Indoors and safe with the loot, we settled on the bed with about twenty little pieces of paper between us. Papers with precarious handwriting reaching out into the world, lost travelers in space. We read them quietly, pausing often to share a look of awe, amusement, confusion. The notes challenged us with their mystique, in the same way Pop challenged us. They were full of magic, of pain, of a struggle to comprehend, to pull together a century.

"*Dear Elizabeth She has done more for me we have a three day ride. Please deer be around becaus I know that you are careful. don't use whiskey. Is it too much to bother? and it is allright that I can not know who I was Some day I will get in trouble.*"

I looked up at Mattie; her eyes were waiting for me. "Trouble?" I asked.

Mattie squinted with her thoughts. "Well, he's a gunfighter...." She read another one. "This one's pretty weird."

"Dear E. to you from Pop. I had an awful Idea. I am not what is Right in some way. I am O.K and will get over soon before any bad mistakes You loving girl of life."

I wondered if Lizzy was watching, reading over our shoulders. And crying, or laughing. "Something's bothering him."

"I sent my horse South nearer Blue. I worked all for it and it is mine. My best for you to keep."

They were like little poems spanning a life fuzzy now with distance. They were secret love letters, and they were the agitated, crazy mutterings I was used to hearing from him every day.

"If you are fond of car cessells has yelow."

Mattie left the room. I sat wondering what a car cessell was. Overwhelmed, I went on the porch and watched my big horseshoes hanging still and silent on the wall. They told me that being heavy was fine and that being a mystery for all time was OK, too. Mattie came up the stairs onto the porch. I wondered where she had been headed.

Her eyes were damp but relieved. "Those notes don't mean anything. Just his confusion."

"I know." The horseshoes echoed my words.

"When Pop met me, it woke up Lizzy in his heart. All those memories are bigger than Pop and his days now." She stared at the low, flat sky. "His mind is really a mess."

"I know."

"It's chaos. Nothing to try to put together."

"I know. It's chaos fixed in its orbit. But he sort of knows what's going on, he's not a goner. Don't short change Pop. He misses Lizzy. And he remembers his horse and his lost mining claim."

Her face softened. "You think?"

"Yeah." I put the notes into my pocket. "He's just a bad writer." I took her hand and smiled; she became lighter. "Let's go put the notes back."

As we rounded the boulder, I realized that the name Blue was becoming a point in the center of the whirling orbit. I quietly tucked Blue away in the corner of my head that was reserving itself for some unknown future need.

17

The moon hung over Bisbee like a white, round sheet alone on a celestial clothesline. I strained my eyes but failed to see a mule's face shining on our heads before we slipped through moonlight and into the mine. We were both reluctant explorers that night, wondering what was in store for us, what could possibly surpass a visit from Elizabeth's spirit. Maybe nothing, but we were definitely nervous. I loved this mine for its secrets, hated it for its surprises.

Mattie threw her voice out in front of her like a shield. "We don't really have to do this. It's one thing to try to find your way without getting lost or falling into a black hole or being flattened under a ton of falling rock. But to then be visited by spirits who leave real physical objects for you...this is creepy."

I couldn't agree more. As we moved along the familiar wall of the main tunnel, I waited for the sweaty mule to return, for Lizzy to appear, for her hat to go flying by. The cool dampness of the rock whispered in my nostrils, and I felt oddly sexual. I imagined my clothes coming off, felt the coolness of the rock on my skin. My body was becoming its own cool-skinned tunnel when I heard Mattie's voice and felt the now-familiar snap back into reality. "The hat's not there."

It wasn't. There was nothing there behind the rock where she had put it before.

"Nice." She was ready to pick a fight with the empty-handed rock. "I guess we are now officially crazy." Did people go crazy together? At the same time? In this case, it seemed possible. But somehow it didn't matter. That hat was around somewhere.

"Relax. We'll see that hat again. Let's keep going." We moved on behind our flashlight. It took us to the side tunnel and to the glistening cavern. I felt our collective relief that the cavern was still there.

No Lizzy, no mule. No hat. Nothing but each other. We sat down to plan our next move. Deeper and deeper into Bisbee's famous cracked hill. I imagined the town in its night life. Silver saloons sloshing beer. Cigarette smoke escaping out of opened windows. Laughter bouncing off the canyon walls, TVs calling out to families, screech owls unheard until bedtime. And two people huddled in the dark down in the Copper Queen, one a little embarrassed.

Mattie was several footsteps ahead of herself. "I think we should go deeper into this tunnel. Look, it keeps going." She threw the light beam past where we sat. We jumped as some bats flapped through the air.

"I used to be able to come in the mine and be completely at peace. Not anymore!" I stood up and breathed deeply to dispel the scare of the bats. "OK. Let's go a little farther. But this is really stupid. We should at least have hard hats on, and some water." Now I was frightened, no bones about it. I grasped Mattie's hand.

The tunnel narrowed a bit, and the sound of dripping water grew distant. I painted the walls and ceiling with the light. They were well timbered. No dirt was falling from above; nothing looked precarious. I filled my chest with a lot of oxygen to combat the tightening grip on my heart. Mattie was quiet.

"Are you breathing?" I whispered.

"Of course I'm breathing," she snapped, as if I had intruded, interrupted something.

I was relentless. "What are you thinking about?"

"Ssh!"

I started to sweat. I smelled the mule again. I squeezed my eyes shut, trying to make the sound of heavy hooves go away. I stopped. I couldn't breathe. I wanted to run back through the tunnel to the big embrace of the waiting moon.

"Oh, God." Mattie had stopped, too. Her words fell with a thud into the dirt.

I opened my eyes and looked down to where she was shining the light. In its bright yellow circle in the dirt lay two big horseshoes.

My eyes grew huge, and I felt like sparking electric wires were spitting from the top of my head. The horseshoes stared up steadily at me, and I stared back in disbelief. I bent down, as if taking a step onto a UFO, touched the dusty metal shoes, and picked them up. They were warm. And they were just like the pair on the wall of my house. I dropped them as the memory of my dream crashed in on me. I saw the four horseshoes falling through the sky. I saw the dead mule above them turning slowly in eternity. The blue sky seemed to fill the dark tunnel. I heard my voice reading the "Mule in the Moon" poem. Then I was sobbing and Mattie was next to me trying to figure out what had happened. The flashlight lay in the dirt, pointing further down the tunnel.

All the way back to the mine entrance I cried. When we got to the little train my waterlogged head found a dry laugh. "What the hell is a car cessell?" I wiped my wet face with the bottom of my shirt and sat in one of the open-sided cars. Mattie climbed in next to me, and I told her my dream about the dead mule with the translucent eyes. And the falling horseshoes. She was quiet, and in the tiniest vagrant moonbeam, I saw that she was smiling. Overcome by her smooth look of love and the deep eyes that sent it, I felt a passion, a sum of a mule's shoes and Lizzy and Mattie and Kate. And safety in the waiting, warm moonlit night just outside. Right there in Turrell's train, I kissed two eyes made of visiting planets, pressed against lips rising from lava, touched a teeming moan in a hot, buzzing swamp.

When we left the train in its dark home, I thought I heard it sigh a dream in which it was flying along a high mountain track through snow and pines, high in the bright sky, free of this dark, lower world.

18

I had put the piece of paper with John Belton's phone number on it under one of my favorite rocks. Petrified wood, actually, a big heavy piece in a special spot on a shelf next to a coyote skull I found out in Tin Star Wash. That place was named after a dead deputy marshall found in it, a long, long time ago. Thea had given me the petrified wood. She got it somewhere up in Utah. I smiled at the memory of her much-appreciated keen eye.

John answered the phone. I spoke quietly, shyly.

"Hi, John, it's Kate. Good. I'm doing good. Uh, can we set up a meeting? Sometime this week?"

When I hung up, I looked around as if I had done something slightly clandestine. As if creeping around in a mine with a flashlight and hallucinating were not clandestine, were normal. It was much more normal to visit a psychic. But I felt sneaky, like I was cheating somehow. Mattie didn't quite get it.

"So you think we have to figure this out on our own? With no help from someone else who probably has a better grip on details from the other side than we do."

I looked at her intently. "The other side?"

"Yeah. Where Lizzy comes from. Where the mule comes from. Don't look at me like that. You know what I'm talking about."

"I know." I paced around the room. "But do you think we're pushing it by seeing John, like we should just let things happen as they will?"

"Look at it this way, Kate," Mattie said with a touch of exasperation, "this is one of those things that just happens."

"I know. But sometimes *this* all seems ridiculous." Mattie looked hurt. "I'm sorry. I guess I'm suddenly not handling it very well."

"If you're doing it, you're handling it." She seemed surprised, as if her words were not her own, and she looked around the room. "Someone made me say that," she declared, quite pleased with herself.

"Well, you're right. It worked, wherever it came from." I went to the petrified wood and slipped John's number back under it, hiding the cheating evidence. "We're going over to John's in an hour. His eyes are really weird, just so you know."

The strong smell of sage met us at the door as John welcomed us warmly into his house. His little shack sat back off the road behind wild, tall, flowery weeds. Old cracked linoleum covered the floor, and there were quite a few chrome-and-vinyl chairs to sit on, each with its share of rips. He had a lot of antlers around, and cactus. No lights were on—just about twenty candles pitching their flames into nervous shadows everywhere. He led us silently to a table in the middle of the room. I noticed a mattress on the floor with thin layers of covers on it in one dark corner of the house. Another corner was a kitchen of sorts. He had a very dirty kitchen for a cook. The counter and sink were burdened with pyramids of dishes and pots that, even in the dim light, showed crusty patches of food that would never scrub off. I imagined a swamp in the sink—stagnant, green-black alligators, sinister vines, sucking mud underfoot. Steam from the tea kettle settled over the scene, turning it into an eery, smoldering, moonlit landfill.

"I have some tea for you," he announced as he sat us down. The table was covered by a worn tablecloth decorated with a faded outline of the state of Arizona with pictures of special places and towns. The huge red-and-yellow letters of ARIZONA stretched out above the northern border. I distracted my discomfort, scanning the map for familiar, safe places that would reassure me of my spot on the planet. Monument Valley, Meteor Crater, Yuma, Fort Defiance, Grand Canyon, Bowie, Tucson, Tombstone, Organ Pipe Cactus, Cochise Stronghold, and Bisbee. By the time the tea arrived, I felt better. John sat down across from Mattie and me, his face just above an army of candles, instantly becoming a Cyclops in their unkind shadows. I glanced at Mattie, whose eyes were closed over the steam of her teacup as it

soothed her face. I was desperate to know what she was thinking.
John spoke to me in a clear voice. "Drink your tea. It will help you open to the possibilities you have brought into the room."

I jerked a glance at Mattie again and found her smiling at me. I sipped the hot, pungent tea. Sassafras. My throat rebelled, but I forced it down. I was the last one to finish. John took the empty cups to the kitchen, added them without a sound to the poised piles, and walked back to the table with his eyes closed.

Mattie took my hand on the tabletop. She seemed just fine with everything. I remembered Mattie telling me a while ago that Baby was enthralled with John and wanted to ask me if she could trade him free meals for psychic readings. Celita let her have it, told her to stay away from John because he believed in strange things and was too old for her. John's soft words pulled me away from my wandering attention.

"I'm not going to do the cards tonight. I feel such strong energies from the two of you, direct possibilities are present. Each of you give me a piece of your jewelry, please."

Mattie immediately pulled off her turquoise ring and handed it to John. The ring had been Lizzy's. She had given it to Mattie just before she died. And of course there was no question for me. I unclasped the chain around my neck on which the small, flat silver horseshoe rested, and lifted it across Arizona to John's waiting hands. The air around my naked neck swirled its discontent.

John held the ring and tiny horseshoe together in one hand. He closed his eyes. Mattie and I waited. I wondered for what. Outside some dogs sang. Someone was laughing all the way down the road. A breeze came through, and the candle flames leaned in unison with it. John's eyes popped open.

"There are many stars in your life together. Old stars that led your past to this junction. Stars known by others gone to the spirit world. You walk a path together now which was cleared for you by another, a woman, a strong woman with great devotion to you both. A relative to one of you—a grandmother?"

Thea used to say that psychics only tell you what you really already know. Mattie's eyes were closed. Her bottom lip trembled.

John continued, the candlelight constantly reshaping his face. "You have fear, but you trust each other, and really, you have to. It's that way. But, you also need to trust something else, something you can't see clearly yet. Wait for it. It is coming. You will know it." He closed his eyes and muttered, "It is something powerful, a powerful energy. It is yellowish in color." His eyes opened and his fingers rubbed back and forth over our jewelry. "Please regard your attitude toward your personal power." He looked at us both. "Find it and believe in it. A yellow light is shining on it. You will see it."

Mattie and I shared a long, new look at each other. The candlelight cupped her face in a twitching glow that excited me. John was speaking, but I couldn't hear his words. I was acutely aware of the sage smell in the room, of the growing sound of the flames whipping around over their candles. Like flags snapping in the wind. I felt enormous, I filled up the room, and the top of my head took off into space. It was a pleasant, peaceful feeling. After what seemed like forever, I settled back into my regular being like a soft exhaling breath and John's voice came to me.

"...afraid because it is the intimate touch of the gracious spirit world."

I wasn't afraid. I wasn't afraid anymore. I hoped it would last.

"Please excuse me," John paused, "but there is a disturbing energy making itself known just a little bit. It will not hinder your journey, but it is part of your journey. It seems like an old man...who is needy. And lost. That is all."

He handed back our warm jewelry, folded his hands in front of him on the tablecloth at Monument Valley, and let out a long sigh. I sank in my chair, speechless and yawning. Mattie stared straight ahead as if in a trance. I put my necklace on and looked around the room. There was no TV, and there were a lot of paperbacks piled around. I looked at John. Who was he? A one-eyed bandit making off with our secret.

"John, thank you. I feel like this will help. Maybe if we need to, uh..." Then my mouth blurted out something totally different from its original intent. "Please tell us how we can find the tunnel we're looking for."

John stared at me for a minute, then cocked his head to the side and asked, "Don't you know another old man?"

The smile on Mattie's face was big enough for all three of us. As we left John behind and maneuvered our way through the weed forest of his front yard, Mattie said, "Everything's going to be fine."

I agreed, not knowing exactly what that meant. The smooth feeling of headless enormity so fresh in my memory followed me down the road. The coyotes saw it, and the fluffed-up owl, and the bats.

19

For the next few days, Carla's face lit up whenever we walked by the hotel desk. I didn't see John around. Carla said he had the flu. It had to be his killer kitchen that got him. I wanted just a glimpse of John daily, to know that he was only a cook in the hotel, a regular guy, madly in love with Carla. And not a Cyclops sent from the other side riding a blind mule. And I was at a loss over Francisco. How were we going to get him to take us to the tunnel, or at least tell us how to find it? All the conversations I had with him in my head came up empty, the winning one always just beyond me.

Mattie seemed content to wait for whatever would happen and spent a lot of time chuckling with Baby and Celita. And Pop. And she was very enamored with me. I always caught her looking at me. We spent most of our days in the cafe now, as if life held only camaraderie and none of the huge mysterious secrets that had been slapping us with apparitions. Celita seemed happy about our renewed presence.

I watched everything, and everyone, and waited. What came was Mr. Randall.

One afternoon, as we followed Pop on his well-worn path to the hotel bar, Carla came running around the corner and ran into all three of us. She untangled herself, backed up a few steps, and held her hands up. "Don't go into the hotel!" Her bird legs were trembling.

"Carla, what's wrong?" I demanded.

"Some old guy from Tombstone says he's here to get Pop."

I spoke calmly. "And what's his name?"

"Randall."

Mattie put a hand to her forehead. "Shit!" We all turned around and went quickly back to the cafe and locked the door. All the customers were gone. Celita walked slowly toward us, wiping her hands on her apron. "What's the matter?"

"Nothing." Celita knew better and kept coming.

"OK, Carla. Tell me exactly what he said to you." Mattie's face slipped on a scowl as she leaned toward Carla.

Carla took a deep, dramatic breath. She spoke in a low voice as she exhaled. "He walked in the door, looked around, then came to the desk, smiled at me, and said, 'Which room is Pop Walker's?' And I said, 'Sir, we do not give out that information.' That was a lie but it just came out that way. Then he turned mean. He said he was worried Pop was sick or in danger, that Pop lived with him and was supposed to be back home by now. He said I'd better tell him where his room was." She threw Mattie a sideways, scared look. "You didn't kidnap that poor old man did you?" She moved in her chair away from Mattie.

Mattie sighed and put her head on the table for a second. "I did not kidnap Pop. He asked me to bring him here, and I don't know why Randall is freaking out. I'll talk to him."

She looked at me, and I answered her silent question. "I'll stay here with Pop."

She and Carla left together. Pop and I stared at each other across the table.

I heard Celita muttering on her way back to the stove, "He can't take Pop. Pop doesn't belong to him, he belongs to us."

Pop opened his mouth just enough to spit out the words, "We're going to the mine."

I nodded slowly. It was true. And we could deal with Randall. Then Mattie walked in with him.

He was a tall, skinny man, with small hands. His eyes were small, too. A frown was chiseled into his granite face, taking up most of the room. When he saw Pop, he took a satisfied breath, but the frown didn't crack. I sat bone still and watched Pop. Mattie waited by the door.

Pop looked up at Randall as he walked over to his chair. They stared at each other in silence before Randall sat down between Pop and me. I looked back at Mattie, who was staring at the floor.

"We're going in the mine," Pop said flatly.

Randall ignored his words. "Everybody's worried about you at home, Pop. I've got your room saved, but you've been gone for three weeks. Why don't I give you a ride home today?" His frown began to falter here and there.

Pop just stared at him with narrowed eyes. After a minute, Randall scratched his head and turned to me. I smiled and shifted in my seat. "I think he's fine here, Mr. Randall. He's got friends and he wants to stay a while longer. He'll be home soon. You don't need to worry."

He spoke, taking his eyes away from mine. He looked around the cafe instead, pausing at Celita, who was leaning on her elbows across the counter, watching. "I think he better come on home with me. He's confused. He doesn't know what he's doing. He has no business here this long."

"It's this long to the end, you aren't here." Pop snapped, surprising Randall, whose head quickly turned back to the table. Celita came over and put a cold can of root beer on the table in front of Pop. He picked it up and took a sip, keeping his eyes on Randall, watching, sizing up the moment with his own whip-cracking thoughts. Celita stood by Pop's chair. We were strategically placed. Well fortified. Now what we needed was for a frenzied Baby to come in, pummeling Randall with her fists.

Instead, Mattie walked slowly toward us, deliberately matching words with steps. "Mr. Randall, as you see, Pop is fine." She stood over Randall's shoulder and put her hands on her hips. "Can I walk you to your car?" He looked up at her, and their eyes were cocked triggers. Pop stopped the showdown. He sprang up from his chair, his eyes juggling in the air. Celita stepped back as he yelled, "Not you! You're not for the mine! You escaped!" He pointed a shaking finger in Randall's face. "I'm with the girls, and the horses are ready." He suddenly calmed, his face relaxed. His hand dropped to his side. "Randall, do you have a cigar?"

Mr. Randall stood up. "No." He looked at Mattie and asked her what she was doing with Pop here. He looked at me. She answered him steadily. "I told you before, Pop asked me to bring him here. We spend a lot of time talking about my grandmother, whom he knew well as a dear friend. We're enjoying a reunion of sorts, and it seems important to him in his own way. We're driving around the countryside, exploring, remembering. We're eating dinner out. He loves the mine. He takes the train tour. There's no reason to take that from him now. No reason. I'm the closest thing he's got to a relative, and he is fine here with me. If he wants to go home with you, no problem. Ask him." She moved over next to me. Randall turned to Pop.

After a short silence, Randall put his hand on Pop's arm and said, "Come on, Pop. Let's get your things. We're going home. We're going to Tombstone. The Crystal Palace." Pop yanked his arm from Randall's grasp and stepped back from him. "No!" He said the word emphatically. Then he looked at me with liquid eyes. "My horseshoes. He can't..." I couldn't understand the rest of the words he muttered. I just smiled and nodded to him. *My horseshoes.*

Randall walked toward the door, and then he was gone. Collectively, except for Pop, our sigh sank into the cool, faded tile floor of our cafe.

The yellow lights from the cafe's ceiling spread out over the empty tables as daylight quietly crept over behind the hills to the west. The only sound around us was the echoing contact of soda cans with tabletop as Celita, Pop, Mattie, and I sat pouting in Mr. Randall's aftermath. Over and over, my memory repeated Pop's voice inside my head: "My horseshoes, my horseshoes, my horseshoes." What had been sparked in his travel-weary brain when he found them in the forgotten dirt of Gleeson? What was hunched over, afraid, hiding in the shadows of his silences, in the narrow stare fixed now on Mattie, unflinching? He stared at her. She and I stared at each other. Celita stared at Pop. We were all connected, by barbed wire, a fence around something that had escaped us.

"Pop needs a shave," announced Celita, either quickly bored or very nervous. The only response was from the song of the soda cans, tinny in their near emptiness.

Celita pushed her chair back and finished her Coke. "I'm going home. You guys are creeping me out." She dragged her feet noisily out the door and let the screen door slam behind her twice.

Mattie put her boots up on Celita's empty chair and lit a cigarette. "Pop," she said as she blew smoke above his head, "tell me something. Do you really want to stay here, with us?" No answer. Mattie pulled her feet down off the chair and leaned close into Pop's face. "Tell me again. Tell me why you want me to take you into that damn mine."

He looked angry. "I knew you'd tell Elizabeth."

Words escaped my mouth when I wasn't looking. "About Blue?" Pop's eyes ripped from Mattie's face and slapped mine. He stood up. "They want my horse. They want my horse!" His hands were trembling. "You go out first." He gestured toward the door and backed away from the table.

"OK." I left the table slowly for the door. I heard the faint rock 'n' roll making its way out of Turrell's bar down the street. Outside, I drew in a huge breath to get me through the rest of my life, looked up and down the street as far as the old setting sun would allow, then went back in. I said, "They got your horse. We'll get them tomorrow, don't worry. You'll have to stay here tonight, in the hotel. We'll walk you down." That would give him something, something to sink his blinking brain into.

Pop was sandwiched between us as our boot heels moved heavily along the wooden sidewalk so used to their weight by now. Pop's bursts of fire were like rapid bullets from his old trusty six-gun, and I loved them. He would sadly melt so soon afterward. I wanted to collect them for him, like spilled pennies from a pocket, so he could remember the passion of Pop Walker, Wyatt Earp's sidekick.

Once in the hotel, Carla's voice was a warm welcome. "Hey, girls. Looks like everything's OK now. That Randall guy was a jerk. Pulled out in his car about an hour ago."

I left my weary partners and went to the desk, leaning toward Carla on the other side. She must've just put a fresh piece of gum in her mouth. I smelled peppermint as Carla's jaw moved in ecstasy. "Carla, thanks for the warning. Thanks for your help," I said quietly, and put a straight finger to my lips to ask her to stop talking just now. She looked slightly offended. I followed Pop and Mattie up the stairs, disappearing at the top in darkness.

The sky had been red, and left behind a dark smear for those of us in Bisbee that night who were still sitting on our porches. *My horseshoes.* I sat alone with them. Pendulous and slightly pink, they held onto a sunset that was already gone. Mattie slept safely inside on the couch. "Our horseshoes," I said out loud, wondering if Pop's sleeping eyes flew open down the canyon at the distant sound of my words. The showdown with Randall had exhausted him, and he escaped into sleep. I pointed my imaginary double-barreled shotgun across the canyon through the stars, one barrel for Mr. Randall and one for Turrell. Ready for the ambush. Ready for this all to disappear as quickly as it had come. No more gristly demented gunfighter. No more loving ghosts, no more red-hot horseshoes. No more dusty coal-eyed lover. I started to cry. The pink was gone from the horseshoes. I set down my weapon, my shield, and went inside to my sweet sleeping lover, tucking myself between her worried, deflated body and the firm protective back of the couch.

The living room was so dark and silent when I woke up from a dream that it felt a little unfamiliar. As I directed a wobbly Mattie from the couch into the bedroom and the cool sheets of the waiting bed, I let my dream visit. A man wearing a hat, sitting on a horse a short distance away, was waving to me. His face wasn't visible, but I knew he was a man. I was curious, wondering who he was as I waved back. He disappeared, and the horse, riderless, walked slowly toward me, getting bigger. Then I woke up.

As the bed pulled me into new sleep, I thought, I hope it wasn't Robert E. Lee and Traveler, come to take me home. I pictured my mother, hands on aproned hips in the doorway of her small, red-brick house surrounded by pine trees and pansies. "Well, I'll be damned," she said, with a big curious smile. "What'd you come home for?"

20

One hundred twelve degrees and as many buzzing, sizzling cicadas pressed the day hotly onto my skin. Pop seemed oblivious. I left Mattie in the cafe to be unhappy with Celita and pulled Pop up the canyon to my house.

We sat in the dehydrating shade, sipping ice tea and staring at the horseshoes together. Pop looked as if he were watching TV. When he first saw them after I sat him in a chair and pointed to them, he smiled. My eyes moved from Pop to the horseshoes and back to him. I had the sense that he would sit there until he died, dead and slumped over, his glass of tea fallen onto the porch, its spreading puddle evaporating into the frying sky.

We had our staring match with the horseshoes for an hour. They won. Footsteps on the stairs leading up to my porch brought me out of my chair, looking for the shining top of Mattie's head to appear.

Instead, the wispy head of John Belton rose in front of me. His hair was the color of a jar of cheap mustard, and his thin pubescent goatee glistened in the sun, defying embarrassment.

"Hi." He stood there as if he were waiting for me to say, "Thank God you're here." A paramedic psychic. Who had called him?

"I hope it's OK for me to stop by." He saw Pop. "Wow." Laughing, he said "Wow" again.

"Sure. Here, have a seat," I said, uncertain. He sat in my chair next to Pop and immediately looked up at the horseshoes. He made no comment. Pop gave him only the slightest glance. Just another day in the twilight zone. I stood at the other end of the porch with my arms crossed in front of me, watching them, not sure I wanted John so close to my private psychic parts. *Get away from my horseshoes.* Why had he come here? Psychics don't do that, I thought. You're supposed to go to them. I gazed out across the canyon and envied a dragonfly's flight over the sleeping, pale sage and mesquite that dotted the canyon's slope.

A low hum came from John's chest and through the line between his thin lips, and his eyes adored the horseshoes. After a few minutes, he looked over at me and said, "Next time you come to see me, bring those horseshoes." Then he resumed his self-appointed vigil.

No. I wouldn't take the horseshoes to him. No way. Fear trembled in my chest. But John was on our side; why did I feel like I was being robbed? Maybe I didn't want this all to end any sooner than it had to.

Pop nodded off to sleep, John seemed to be sending a trance signal to the horseshoes, and I realized the phone was ringing.

"Janice?"

"That's what I said."

"I'm sorry. I guess I'm just surprised." And I was. Today was not a good day. Two too many unanticipated, unclear people showing up.

"Well, that's too bad. I haven't forgot you two girls. But I don't know what to do. I can't help you. I haven't seen you around and I wondered how you're doing." She sounded oddly frantic. I shut my eyes.

"I haven't seen you around either. How are you?" I waited.

"Not so good, really. I mean, life can be the pits, you know."

"Kind of like the world's largest open pit mine?" My lack of sympathy went unnoticed.

She laughed. "Have you figured out how to get in that tunnel?" The words crept out of her mouth reluctantly.

"Interesting you should ask. I just this minute figured it out. Just now."

"No kidding!"

"Yeah. I have a retired mule in my back yard, used to work in the mine, and I'm going to take it in there and let it lead me to the tunnel. By memory. Mules have good memories."

"What on earth are you talking about?"

"That's what I'm going to do. Right now. Gotta go." I hung up. I hung up on Janice after telling her a lie. I was turning mean. I went anxiously over to the window to see Pop still asleep and John's eyes glued to the air. For some reason his eyes looked further apart today. Maybe it was the light. And Janice. Maybe she felt bad about being too chicken to help us. She was reaching out, and I practically spit in her face. I paced around the room like an ornery house cat. The phone rang again. It was Janice.

"Kate? Wait. I want to come. I'll be at your house in ten minutes. Don't leave." She was gone, and the dial tone laughed into my ear.

This was not a good day. I took a long, deep, excruciating breath and put the phone back on the receiver. I didn't want Janice to come over here. What the hell was wrong with her? Maybe I should just leave the house. I went onto the porch and stood in front of John, not knowing why. He looked up at me. What had I wanted to say? My breathing quickened, and John's eyes moved back closer together. I turned and scooted back into the house, a squirrel changing its mind in the middle of the highway.

The phone felt like a weapon in my hand as I called the cafe.

"Baby, hi. Let me talk to Mattie." When I heard the truest, brightest voice these hills had ever heard, my head cleared. "Hey, you've got to get up here, fast. No, he's fine. I'm OK. Just come up here, it's much too complicated to begin to explain."

Mattie beat Janice by one minute, so that when Janice arrived, dressed for adventure in her tight jeans and Keds, Mattie didn't really have the true impact of my quick story about John's visit and Janice's phone call. John had nonchalantly said hello to both of them. All the activity on the stairs woke up Pop, who appeared in the living room requesting a whiskey. I took his shoulders and gently turned him back to the porch and the horseshoes. "I don't have any whiskey. Your turn to keep watch. Don't fall asleep." He snapped into his guard duty with two hard, invincible eyes.

I looked at Mattie and Janice, both waiting in anticipation— Janice for directions, Mattie for an explanation. Somehow I knew I would disappoint them both. Janice looked around and out the window to the back of the house. "Where's the mule?" My wayward smile stalled for time. I think Mattie understood I was lost.

"So, let's go. Let's go see Francisco." She took my arm and led me out the door. Janice followed. Mattie stopped and yelled to Pop and John, "Come on, we're going to Francisco's."

On some simmering level I knew that Mattie had picked up the trail and was taking the craziness and the configuration of the moment in her tight fist and thrusting it into the very near future. I was surprised the horseshoes didn't hop down off the wall and follow us across the canyon to Francisco's. But as we walked, I swear I could hear their heavy steps echoing between my ears.

His house looked hot to the touch, the faded, smooth wood thin and brittle. Mattie knocked on the door. We all waited as if we knew what we were doing. A tiny creek of sweat ran down each of my temples and evaporated below my jaw. Cicadas surrounded us, and their eerie buzzing called Francisco out to his door.

When I saw his tired, deeply lined face frowning at the crowd on his doorstep, I realized I missed him at the cafe.

"Francisco, hi. We need to talk to you. We need your help." Mattie didn't stop as we walked through the door. "You are the only person in this whole town who can help us." When we got to the kitchen, she asked John and Pop and Janice to wait in the living room, then shut the door. "They are as concerned as we are, but there's no need to bombard you with all of us about this." The three of us sat down at the table. Francisco was still frowning.

"OK. I know you don't ever want to go back in the Copper Queen. But you have got to tell us how to get to Tunnel 3. Just describe how to find it. The reason is simple. It means life or death for Pop. I can't sit by and watch him wither away with the pain of people he's lost. He needs to find it all again. All of them. Lizzy, Wyatt—"

"And Blue," I interrupted. Francisco's frown hardened as he shot me a quick look. I would fish for Blue every chance I got.

He leaned back in his chair and said slowly, "Then go to the cemetery."

"*I* know they're dead. But *he* doesn't really know that, I guess. Listen, please." She changed her tactic and leaned across the table toward Francisco. "I'm not leaving this house until you tell me how to get to that tunnel." Her eyes darkened fiercely. "Pop believes that he absolutely must go into that tunnel, and I'm here to see that he does. You have to help us."

Francisco smiled. "He can go there. He knows the way. But it is not safe maybe. I don't know."

I sat up straight in my chair. "Wait a minute! Pop knows the way? What are you talking about? What do you mean?"

Mattie's eyes narrowed as we waited. Francisco was silent. She said, "You're saying he's been in there before? Well, even so, his memory is shot full of holes. He can't take us, we have to take him."

I felt tears come to my eyes. Now what watery source was visiting? What mystical spin, what head-stealing news was waiting behind the sun out there? I knew Pop had been in that mine.

Francisco's voice broke through my tears, describing a tunnel off the main one that had a large area mined, like a cavern, on the left wall.

We all marched across the canyon, backlit by the ponderous shape of a gold sun, like a troupe of Halloween adolescents too big for our costumes, mourning the sun's slow departure. We didn't listen to Janice's incessant whining: what was going on and where was the mule and wasn't it too dark now? I thought of the stars, of our guiding stars. They had known all along. I should have realized when we found the horseshoes in that tunnel. But that would have been assuming too much. Francisco said it was a long tunnel. So we would have to go further. My excitement battled with my still-seeping tears. We had to get rid of these tagalongs. But I wondered if this would have happened without them. I took Mattie's hand as we neared my house.

Everyone said their goodnights as if we were leaving a party. Pop was smiling. Mattie left to drive him down to the hotel, and I was alone on the front porch in a stirring breeze. There were the horseshoes, still and strangely bright in the sun's last sigh. Ghosts. If I took them into the tunnel to meet their other half, would they produce the mule? Magical thoughts tricked me into laughing. Tricked me into believing everything I believed. Where was Mattie?

Now it was dusk. Now it was no fun. Now we could take Pop into the tunnel. Then something good would happen to him, then Mattie would leave and take him back to Tombstone, then she would go back to her long-lost ranch and her horses. I heard her running up the stairs and she filled up the new night in front of me and I was surrounded by her. She kissed my head as she held it close to her chest, and we rocked like that, there on the porch in front of the pulsing eyes of the ghost mule's shoes.

"I'm not going to just leave," she announced loudly. I pulled my head up from her arms to look as far as I could into the swirling dusk in her eyes. "What?"

"I can't just leave." She pulled away a little. "What's going to happen?" She was growing frantic. Up in the big sky the stars were rushing in to help. Reinforcements.

I took her hands into mine and said gently, "It doesn't matter what happens." And I smiled, "Just don't leave."

Her head turned to the sky and her heavy sigh fell to the porch, sending the worn boards into a creaking frenzy. The deep blue twilight above us turned to black as I leaned back against the wall of my trusty porch. Mattie settled in next to me, our shoulders pressing in a long, still kiss.

"Orion's always first," she said to the fresh night sky with its three lined-up stars trailing down toward us.

I gazed dreamily upward. "Yeah. You and me and Orion, dangling above the porch, just dangling and burning up light." Mattie's hand came over, and my knee oozed like butter under its touch, inside the protective cup of her palm. She turned and faced me, both of my knees at her mercy. A slow gasp traveled up the center of me, splitting me in two, widening a path to my mouth. When she kissed me, the gap snapped shut, catching her inside, trapped, like Wyatt Earp, a prisoner behind bars of ribs.

"See, now it'll never be over." My words came fast, certain. I kissed Mattie like a summer flash flood gobbling up a rickety town. "There's no 'I was in love with a woman from Bisbee once….'" I pulled her shirt up over her head and it landed in soft folds on the porch. Her sparkling eyes swept my face and lit up what we knew. Where we were going. I shut my eyes to the blinding light, letting my mouth find its way onto her demanding breasts, my skin giving way to her hands under my shirt, under my jeans, to the passing of breezes brushing where her hands had been as my clothes jumped off my body. Never had a porch heard such a chorus of creaking boards. Never had Bisbee's moon risen faster to see it all. Never before this night had I swallowed myself whole.

The moonlight slowed us, stretched us across the porch, illuminating each goosebump, each trail of traveling fingers. We pulled up our muscles and opened our dams and shouted through the roof, shouted to Orion, who heard us and smiled.

"I'm never leaving you," Mattie whispered into my tangled pile of hair. The stars above relaxed and settled into place in the sky as the night dropped over our bodies like a worn, soft sheet. "I'm keeping you right here." Her arms surrounded me, softly, triumphantly, and she kissed my neck and shoulders, calling all the levitating parts of me back to my body. She held me, and I hibernated for a while in her arms. After a long time, when the moon was way across the sky, I sat up stiffly. Bones that had been competing with floorboards clicked back into place, and I gathered my clothes and my boots into a pile at my side.

"I can't do this. I can't make a fist. Can't get my clothes back on. Oh boy." My head was swimming, my heart content to just meander slowly through my veins.

Mattie murmured that sure I could. I could continue my life even though it had stopped for thirty minutes on another planet right in the middle of alien sex. We stood up and slipped smooth limbs into wrinkled cotton. We laughed. The stars took our boots and ran off with them.

Just as I was about to suggest going inside, my head started tingling and my heart raced against itself to some faraway finish line. Mattie started shaking.

"I'm cold. Why am I cold?" She crossed her arms over her chest and rubbed her bare arms, as if trying to start a fire with the taut, fleshy sticks. "It's cold." She looked at me for an answer, but I was on my way out of my body. I felt the inside of myself coming up from my feet through my stomach and squeezed my eyes shut to keep me inside myself. I gripped Mattie's arm to help keep my feet on the porch and was about to scream when it all ended with a snap. My eyes opened as I heard Mattie make a sound with her mouth and felt her take a step back.

"Kate." Time stopped. Orbits stopped. And all the crickets, at once.

"I see her." A dusty Elizabeth, looking pained and worn, stepped toward us, with the horseshoes in her hands. We backed up to the edge of the porch. My heart seemed to squeeze itself out of my rib cage and hid somewhere nearby. I felt the empty hole, the exposed bones. I was caving in when suddenly she disappeared and I heard Mattie breathing fast, saying "Lizzy" over and over. I realized I was holding something in my hand and looked to see my fingers curled around a horseshoe. The other one was in Mattie's hand. Up on the wall of my steady house were two nails, temporarily relieved of their burden.

21

The next morning seemed impossibly brighter and clearer, inventing a surreal desert landscape for my little creaky town. The sagebrush dotting the way out of town blazed like Moses' burning bush. Long morning shadows raced across the flats, never quite reaching the mountains. The day's first breezes danced through the dusty streets, giving everyone a little pat on the back hello. Something smelled good, like cedar, like the night's leftover evaporation.

Just to defy this crisp goodwill, the first customer in the cafe was Turrell. But you couldn't really call him a customer: I made him leave. He bumped into the second customer as he walked backward to the door, sneering at me. The second customer was Francisco, followed by Baby. Celita, busy at the stove, had ignored Turrell as he stated loudly that he wanted to talk to Pop. Now she called over to me, "Bad way to start the day."

"Not so bad. Glad to see Francisco here," I said as I nodded a greeting to him. He sat down with Pop and Mattie as I walked out to the sidewalk. No sign of Turrell. The sun was beginning its climb up the sky, and the cicadas were tuning up. Mattie came out of the cafe and lit a cigarette.

"What do you think Turrell wants to talk to Pop for?"

"Well, my guess is that he wants Pop to tell him where his buried treasure is. Think of it. Turrell would be rich. He could quit his job. He could move to Las Vegas, buy some fancy clothes and a bolo tie, drink good whiskey, and gamble his life away." I looked from the street to Mattie. "See, he's motivated."

She laughed and tucked her hand in the back pocket of my jeans. We stood there on the sidewalk, saying hello to anyone who walked by, stepping aside for customers making their way into the cafe. We looked at each other off and on, checking in, making sure we were who each thought the other was. Little smiles, sighs, a few questioning eyes. Fidgeting boots, arms with nothing to do. Memories of a special ghost and two cowgirls shooting silver stars at a mule in the moon.

A car pulled up and parked in front of us. It was Janice's Oldsmobile, and she climbed out in a white sundress. Her eye makeup was smeared under her eyes like smudges of charcoal. And her eyes were red. As she came even closer, I saw that wet smears held to her upper lip under her nostrils. We both stared at her as her dust settled.

"Hi—" She couldn't say the rest of her words as she inhaled her tears.

Mattie put a hand on her arm. Janice's fist squeezed a damp baby-blue Kleenex tightly.

"What's wrong, Janice? What happened?" The gentleness of Mattie's voice set Janice off, and she told us a sketchy, slobbery story. Her bird Koko had died. Maybe Billy had killed it, or at any rate, he was glad the bird was dead. Ronnie wouldn't talk. The little thing was so soft and light and its head hung down so low when she picked its body up from the newspaper and took it out of its cage. She had cried and cried and no one would pay any attention to her. She screamed and no one came. Koko was in the car. How had it happened? She woke up to a beautiful day, went into the kitchen to make coffee, heard no singing. She pulled the nighttime towel off the cage to find the lifeless, silenced bird on the bottom.

"Come on. Let's go to my room." Mattie turned Janice in the right direction as I peeked into the car to see a little bundle wrapped in a dishtowel on the passenger seat. My eyes stung.

"Janice." She turned to look at me. "We can have a funeral."

Her ragged eyes knew I was right, and they let new tears spurt out. I followed a few steps behind the two of them as they trudged arm in arm up the hotel steps.

Janice's cigarette smoke hurt her spent eyes and brought her evil thoughts. She sat on Mattie's bed and said all she could see was

Billy's decapitated head stuffed in the bird cage. She hated him. She couldn't go back to that house. She hated Ronnie because he was just a little Billy. She thought to blow up the hardware store with dynamite.

Mattie brought a wet washcloth from the bathroom and made Janice lie back on her bed and hold the moist warmth to her closed eyes. Her cigarette died in the ashtray on the table next to the bed. I stood by the window, hoping to catch a breeze. Mattie came over to me as Janice caught up with her breath and her body sank into the mattress.

"Poor Janice," Mattie muttered.

"Poor Koko," I said.

The wind picked up outside. Some kids were playing soccer with a beer can. I thought maybe we'd have a storm. "It's going to rain."

Mattie glanced at me curiously as I walked away from the window. Janice was quieting down. I watched her creased sundress try unsuccessfully to hide her vulnerability. The washcloth lay heavy over her eyes, probably cold by now, losing its purpose with each cruel moment.

"Janice," I said firmly, "are you OK? Can I talk to you?" There was no response. I sat on the edge of the bed, and her sad body tilted slightly toward me in the slope I made. "Janice." I poked her shoulder gently. "Janice."

She sat straight up in a flash and whipped the washcloth away from her face, revealing smoldering red-hot eyes and the meanest mouth I'd ever seen. I almost fell off the bed. Her breasts pushed heavily against the constraint of her dress as her breaths grew quicker. We were a foot apart. I felt Mattie suddenly there behind me. Janice's face grew pink and her eyes moved up to Mattie, over my head. They still smoldered, like the barrels of two just-fired six-guns, one in each fist, up in the air for everyone who was watching to see. They followed Mattie as she lowered herself slowly to the edge of the bed next to me. We sat like that, silent, motionless, for a good three minutes. Then I saw the fire go out. Her breasts disappeared in a long sigh; her head sank down. I wanted to put my hand on her head, to help support it. But I couldn't. Mattie did. Janice folded the washcloth into a neat package and handed it to me. I remembered the bundle on the seat of her car and what I had come over to ask her. I whispered her name, risking the six-guns, but this time she answered a pathetic, "What?"

"We can bury Koko at my house, under the mesquite tree in

the back. He'd pretty much be in the shade except in early morning. We can do that. Today."

New tears splashed on her hands in her lap. "He loved to be on the porch in the sun then. About eight o'clock, every Sunday, I'd put him there." She wiped her hidden cheeks. "One time Ronnie knocked over his cage. He bumped into it on his way running out the door. I was so mad at him."

All of Lowell must've heard her scream that day, must've known her boy was bad, must've heard Koko shriek in terror as his cage tumbled through the world.

"Did Koko ever ride in the train?" I asked.

Mattie gave me one of her astonished looks at my bizarre question. She jumped up from the bed.

"You want to do that Janice, bury Koko at Kate's?" Mattie's urgency moved Janice from the bed, bent and beaten. Her answer was a shaking hand on the doorknob, leading us down the hall in her twisted, wrinkled dress, her sandals slapping against the bottom of her heels. We moved down the stairs, following Janice's hanging head in silence, to find Carla's waiting stare at the bottom.

"Who died?" she asked, holding her breath. Death in Bisbee was a chance for the town to relax by a molecule, and one more opportunity to prepare. Everyone rose to the occasion in collective fashion, bearing personal items to rest around the particular mound of dry earth. Gifts to vanished bodies and lingering souls. Deaths were moments of acceptance of some deeper open pit, recognition of our very own slippage.

"Janice's bird," I whispered. Carla let her breath out, and her face told me that bird deaths do not count. *Yes they do.* Outside, thunderheads were gathering for an afternoon foray.

I wanted to bring Pop along. "Can we stop in the cafe and get Pop?" I asked as I stepped next to Janice on the sidewalk.

Janice nodded, her head still hanging, her chin lined up directly with her cleavage. When it rained later, she would be cold in her sundress. I knew it would rain.

I got Pop and told Celita what we were doing.

"A funeral for a bird?" She shook her head and turned her back to us, laughing. Her irreverence was a cover for her fear of what this would do to the woman she babysat for, to the woman we all hated to love. I was glad I knew that, and turned toward the funeral march with Pop.

We climbed out of Mattie's jeep and went around to the back of the house. Janice asked me to carry Koko's still bundle to the tree. Towering clouds peered down over their protruding bellies and watched our tiny, faraway funeral. Mattie dug a hole with a little garden shovel, struggling against the hard, rocky ground. Sweating, and stabbing, she managed to produce a grave. A bird-sized grave under the delicate umbrella of the lacy leaves of an old, loyal mesquite. I watched Pop as he looked at the top of Mattie's head. He looked like the tree. His lips were moving. His silent, delicate words were all around us. Mattie stood up stiffly from her labor and wiped away a tear with the back of her soiled hand, leaving a black mourning stripe under one eye. She glanced at Janice, who was growing a stern, bitter face. I held out the bundle to Janice as the sky darkened. Her mouth tightened. She held Koko, light as air, and knelt down next to the hole. The bundle was too big to fit.

Mattie knelt next to Janice and said, "Koko needs some freedom. Let's take him out and give him to the soil." Janice resisted.

"It's the dishtowel," I said, and ran into the house and grabbed a yellow bandanna. When I handed it to them, Janice gave the bundle to Mattie, who pulled away the towel and unveiled Koko's still body. Janice let out a muffled shriek. Mattie's earthy hands gently wrapped him in the bandanna and put him down in the hole. He fit. Janice was immobile.

After Mattie and I covered the hole with dirt, I stuck a feather I had, from a crow, in the top of the little mound. We sat looking at the grave, at the elegant black tombstone, until a drop of rain landed squarely on the top of the feather, jolting it. Thunder raced across the sky above us, and the temperature dropped. The air was gray. "Take me back to my car, I'm cold," Janice said, her voice empty, dry.

"Maybe you shouldn't drive in the storm—"

"Please, take me back."

Pop wouldn't leave the grave. He wouldn't come in out of the rain. Mattie brought Janice to her car for a hellish drive back to Lowell. Lightening dropped its frenzied bolts over Bisbee. I stayed with Pop, under the tree, over Koko's grave. Pelted by big drops. It was as dark as an eclipse. He wouldn't budge, just stared down at the mound with the sorry-looking drenched feather holding its own in the downpour. Rain gushed off the brim of his hat like a gutter along the roof of a house and hit Koko's grave with a waterfall. Lightning struck everywhere but inside of us. My dry, warm house was only a few feet away, but I couldn't leave him there by himself, an old lightning rod out for one last, daring thrill.

Wind slapped against us, and sheets of rain moved down my body in rushes. I smelled the water and the creosote bushes out there, everywhere. This is what it was always like for unmoving things—boulders, houses standing still in the swirl. Waiting. Eroding. Now Pop and I were statues, or at least we were until Mattie's newly arrived voice said we weren't.

"Goddamnit! Both of you, get in the house!" She grabbed my arm and Pop's and ripped us from our roots, practically throwing us through the door. The last thing I remember seeing before a towel engulfed my head was a little moat, full of water, around Koko's mounded grave. I thought soon the grave would start to float, in the runoff, down the canyon, the tattered crow feather as its sail. With Koko hidden inside like a Pharaoh, safe in his tomb.

Mattie scrubbed my naked self raw with that towel, cussing the whole time. I made her stop.

"Where are my clothes?"

"Outside."

"Where's Pop?"

"In the bathtub."

"In the bathtub? In my tub?" I couldn't picture it.

Mattie lit a cigarette and looked at me from a distance. "You're next," she said with authority.

Pop sat in the kitchen drinking coffee in my bathrobe. My skin was warm and damp from a scalding bath, and dry clothes caressed it softly. Outside, the rain was gone, the air full of new clean sunshine, warming as it dried. Like me and Pop. I was afraid to look at Koko's grave, expecting to see a hole, a puddle. But the mound was there, and Mattie was firming it up with her hands, straightening out the feather. The sun picked up the curve of her back, the vertebrae of her neck. This had truly been a crazy day. But she would make it end like any other.

That night I dreamt into the back of Mattie's head, so close to my warm breath. It was the man on the horse again, with the hat on, still unrecognizable. Sleepy afterthoughts said maybe it wasn't a horse, and not a man, but Elizabeth on a mule. No, it wasn't Elizabeth, somehow I knew it was a man. A man on a—mule. My head jerked up off the pillow. It was a mule! Groaning, I rested my head again slowly on the pillow. Mattie turned over on her back, still asleep. A deflating moon sent shadows into the room, and they settled down at the foot of the bed. I never really went back to sleep but struggled the rest of the night to keep safely inside myself.

    When Mattie woke up, I was relieved to see her doughy face so close to mine, smiling in the morning sun.

22

"We should call Janice, see how she is. I want to get her another bird." Mattie poured coffee for us on the porch. "A big parrot. They live a long time."

Koko certainly didn't die of old age. The memory of the little parakeet's limp body made me look over to its grave. Still there. I felt a certain responsibility having the grave under my tree. A certain role, a certain obligation, to the other side.

We sat together, watching the rooftops of Bisbee in the morning stillness. It seemed we were the first ones up. I remembered my dream.

"I'm being haunted by a mule."

Mattie's eyes narrowed and her face stilled. "What mule?"

"The mule who left those goddamn horseshoes on my front porch." I took a deep breath to still the rising frustration in my throat. "The mule poem in that book, the mule I dream about, the mule I imagined, or didn't imagine, in the mine that time we saw Lizzy."

Mattie looked confused.

I nodded. "There was a mule there, before we saw Lizzy standing there with her hat. The mule was there, like a part of me, walking just ahead of us. I saw its butt. I smelled its sweaty hide. I heard its hooves hitting the dirt...." My voice trailed off out over the canyon.

Mattie got up, went to the porch railing, and turned around to look at me folded limply in my chair. "What do you dream?"

I reluctantly let out the image of the man on the mule. "I realized last night it's a mule, not a horse."

"You can't see his face?"

"No."

My phone was ringing, and I let it. I left it inside to scream and scream for me in vain.

"Kate." She came over to me and knelt in front of me, her hands on my bare, vulnerable knees. "I dreamt last night about a man with a hat on holding a candle out to us. We were in the mine. I couldn't see his face. He was just a silhouette."

After a dumb pause, she let out a laugh and slapped her hands down on my knees. "We're going to the mine tonight," she said with finality as she pulled me up out of my chair and kissed me.

"With Pop?" My words were feeble.

"No, not yet. Just us."

We walked to the hotel as the rest of the town woke up. Carla stopped us as we headed for the stairs to Pop's room.

Mattie was alarmed. "What? Is he gone?"

"No, no honey. I just wanted to show you something he gave me last night. He came out of the bar just before I left, gave me this note, and went upstairs. I made sure he went into his room. Anyway, look at this crazy thing."

Mattie unfolded the piece of paper, and the three of us looked at the words together.

Dear E he is dead you know I am sorry. Four of your people know. You are in the dirt. Come back soon we can ride out. Bring water.

"God—" Mattie folded the paper up and asked Carla if she could have it.

"Of course you can have it. What do you think it means?"

"Doesn't mean a damn thing," I said authoritatively as I took Mattie's arm and headed for the stairs. "Thanks, Carla."

Something about Koko's funeral had set him off. Mattie agreed. When we knocked on his door it opened immediately. He was ready for whatever, hat on, waiting at the door. "Mornin'," we muttered, as he quickly went through the door past us. I felt angry at him because I couldn't know what thoughts swirled under that hat. Because I couldn't know what mystery drove him, or what mystery pulled him.

Francisco was sitting at a table when we walked in the cafe. Baby was setting tables, and Celita wasn't there. "Where's Celita?" I said as I looked around.

Baby answered as she placed clean salt-and-pepper shakers around the room. "She's gonna be a little late. Said she was up late over at Janice Beecham's last night. I brought Grandpa over. She'll be here soon. I'll get the coffee going."

Mattie and I flipped our curious eyes at each other. "I'll get the coffee, Baby," Mattie said as she walked away, leaving her eyes with me. I stood in the middle of the floor, lost, until I heard the unmistakable sound of Pop and Francisco talking to each other. Having a conversation. In a fit of opportunism, I sauntered over to their table to listen. Of course, this stopped them. I sat down, apparently unwelcome, across from their now-silent postures. I wondered if they had been having conversations only when no one was listening. Celita came through the door in a late rush, ordering Baby around before the door closed behind her. I went over to her as she put her apron on behind the counter.

"Everything's under control. Relax. How's Janice?"

"Beats me. I was there last night, and she was passed out on the couch the whole time. Guess she got real drunk and Mr. Beecham had to go somewhere. So he called me to sit with Ronnie." Her voice was drowned out by the noisy preparations in the kitchen. Suddenly she stopped and turned to me. "He's a real asshole. He took my arm and squeezed it 'til it hurt and told me not to tell anyone, not one person, about it." She opened the cooler and began throwing the day's food out onto the counter. "Asshole."

Why would anyone murder a parakeet? Maybe Ronnie did it. Maybe Koko had heart failure. For that matter, just how well did we know Janice?

I sat there in silence with my old scruffy mystery men while the cafe grew busy and its sounds settled between my ears. Koko's soul lifted itself through tiny ribs and clumps of dirt and spun up into the sky. I thought I felt it pause momentarily over the cafe.

A while later John Belton came in and sat next to Pop, who smiled at him as if they'd arranged this particular rendezvous. I heard Mattie laughing at the counter with someone.

"How is everybody today?" John's voice seemed to bounce on the tabletop.

I shifted in my seat. "Well, I feel especially tricked into thinking that I'm having a normal day in a normal small town surrounded by normal people. How 'bout you?"

John just nodded, without any more words.

"You want Baby over here? Hungry?"

"No thank you, Kate. I just dropped by to see if you wanted me to give Pop here a reading."

My face jutted out toward his. "No I do not." I just let myself be mean.

The screen door flapped behind me as the heat begged me to come out into it. It motioned to me with its fiery fingers and its scorching breath, said it had something to show me. I stood considering a long walk, considering sneaking away, considering no sound and no intrusion but that of the crackling cicadas. So, I stepped out into the street and stretched my arms to the vast Sonoran desert, my back to every other thing.

Heading west through Bisbee's tiny expanse, I passed the American Legion building and turned up the old stage road. Dry heat shrunk my temples, and my lips tingled as I came up on the town cemetery. I stopped. No one was around, and few cars struggled up the winding hill. The cemetery was on a hillside, a slanted tumble of broken tombstones and faded wooden crosses. One corner held a large marble mausoleum. The Grady family. All of them, for generations. I hadn't been up here in a long time but I remembered the iron door with its glass barred window and the eight drawers of dead Gradys, four on each side. Grady was a big mine family. A Copper King with his fifty grandchildren, spread all over the southwest. There was no room for those grandchildren in this tomb. They would grace the green cemetery lawns of Tucson, Albuquerque, Phoenix.

Then there was an area of manicured Christian graves with little lambs and angels standing watch in stone. Store owners, librarians, teachers, contractors, ranchers. The rest of the cemetery was poor, plain. Miners, outlaws, prospectors. And their women, and their babies. I walked up to them, following the beckoning hands of the heat. Some lucky soul had a mother come by recently with flowers. A plastic rosary hung from a splintered cross stuck fast in the hard desert earth. Next to it was an odd tombstone made of wood. I bent over to get a better look at it. As I saw the name, I felt my blood evaporate into the hot, dry air.

Jack "Blue" Timmins
October 5, 1879–May 12, 1920

My first impulse was to run, but having no blood, I sank slowly onto my knees in front of the grave. The hot hardness of the sacred spot rose up through my bones. My hands found my face, my eyes squeezed tight until they hurt.

After a while, I relaxed into a sitting position and faced the worn gray marker. We looked each other squarely in the eye. I told the empty grave what I knew. "Mr. Blue Timmins," I said, finally, "what happened in that mine?"

The day grew wispy as high, flat clouds picked up their pace across the sky prairie. My feet pulled me away from the cemetery and back toward town. A noisy crow followed me, hopping from high branch to telephone wire to rooftop, and the wind pulled at my hair behind me. I wasn't sure whether I was annoyed or afraid. I pushed my breath out to the rocks, the little houses, and the trees as my boots hit the firmness of the old road. I did not want to go into the mine that night.

As I passed by the hotel, I noticed Mattie sitting on the porch, tipping back her chair as far as she could without falling over backward. She rocked slightly, tempting the tip-over. Her face was bored. I walked heavily up the steps onto the porch, and her eyes watched me without moving her head from its straight-ahead position. When I stopped in front of her, her eyes were dug in and wouldn't be budged.

After a respectable amount of time I announced, "I have something to show you."

Mattie let the chair come forward from its tilt with a thankful thud and stood up, ready. She was always ready. She seemed to know instinctively when some incredible thing was twisting around in my eyes. I had come to rely on her waiting readiness because it gave me time, and trust. I turned toward the steps as she fell in behind me. On the sidewalk, an unexpected thought stopped me: Pop had to come. He had to see the grave. I had to see him see the grave. "Let's take the jeep and get Pop."

Pop mumbled on the drive, his eyes darting around the landscape like a hawk. Mattie and I rode in silence, bouncing stiffly over the cracks and ruts in the old road. The cemetery appeared under the scattered white clouds, harsh against the blue sky around it. "Stop here," I said quietly, and Mattie cut the engine, taking in the simple tombstones with watery eyes. I turned and looked at Pop in the back seat. He was staring at me. The familiar cosmic confusion swirled in his eyes, and I suddenly felt intensely responsible for these two for an eternity. I gently guided them through the faded crosses to the gray wooden marker. Pop seemed particularly feeble, his body creaking in its stiff maneuvering. I stopped them and pointed to the marker at our feet. Mattie stared at it, her eyes overflowing with the information. She turned slowly to Pop, and her eyes filled with him and the realization that Pop knew the legendary mine ghost. She looked ready to reach for her holster. Flames flew up in her eyes as she backed away from Pop a few steps. She tried to speak as new breath pumped through her chest, but no words came. Pop bent toward the flat wooden tombstone. His fingers gripped it like bones reaching from the lost dark to touch something familiar from life. He froze there, bent like that, a fallen crooked branch leaning against the marker.

There we were, like the frozen statues in Tombstone of the Earps and the Clantons, guns drawn, in the OK Corral. There we were, after-hours, when the show was over and the tourists gone. The cemetery's breezes flicked our hair, and the old plastic rosaries hanging on crosses tapped their hosts to the wind's snappy rhythm.

A spirited gust lifted Pop's hat off, sending it up against Timmins' neighbor to the left. Pop straightened and set out to retrieve his hat. A look of great sadness filled each long crack and crevice of his face. Bending carefully, he picked up his hat, put it on, and stared out over the monumented world and far beyond.

Mattie was now heading back to the jeep.

"Pop, let's go." I waited for him to join me, and we wound our way through the graves, leaving them to the waning day and the promise of another heavy, blue twilight.

We drove back to the hotel through jolting silences on the rugged road. Mattie headed straight for the hotel bar. She sat Pop down and slammed a glass of whiskey on the table in front of him. Never taking my eyes off Mattie, I sat down very slowly in my chair between the two of them. Mattie lit a cigarette and looked up at the handsome old ceiling, at everyone else's smoke swirling under the dim light. Then her eyes came crashing down on Pop. Their dark sharp fall demanded of Pop what he couldn't produce. Who was Jack "Blue" Timmins to Pop?

She spoke with a voice that held back a raging flash flood. "Pop, Kate and I are going to talk about this Timmins thing, this Blue thing.

If you have anything to offer, jump in."

Her face then shifted to deliberately settle in with mine. Mattie's jet black eyes touched my spine, and they were moist, glistening. She took several noticeable breaths but failed to speak. I stepped in.

"So Pop knew Jack Timmins. Pretty weird." I looked at Pop. He was not looking at us, his head turned away in stiff-necked profile. "Figure that one out. I suppose he's got him confused with Wyatt Earp. That never made sense anyway. Makes me feel better."

Mattie watched my eyes with a liquid gaze that left the room, left Bisbee. "Did I tell you Lizzy was a rodeo star? Best barrel racer in Arizona. That's one of my great disappointments, that I never saw her ride in the rodeo. I have pictures of her, though." She paused. "You'll see them, when I get back to the ranch. I want you to see them."

My heart kicked me in the ribs just in case I had missed the moment. My joy was silent, discreet. I smiled into eternity, as the sounds in the bar slowly drifted up through the roof and disappeared into the starry night sky.

"Where is Blue? When do we go?" Pop's glass was empty much sooner than usual, and his low voice pulled us away from each other. We both turned and looked at him and said "What?" at the same time.

"Where?" It was all he could say. Finding Blue's grave didn't do a thing for Pop's confusion. Why should it? His brain was far beyond being stuck in a confusing set of circumstances. Mattie and I were the ones stuck, confused. I looked at Mattie.

"Pop knew Jack Timmins. Pop rode with Wyatt Earp. Pop was a prospector, your grandmother's lover. Pop wants to go in the mine. Lizzy's spirit visits us." I heard a loud click inside my head. "And that man on the mule, the one in the mine with the candle in the dreams, that's Blue! It's Jack Timmins!"

"Or Wyatt Earp," Mattie laughed.

"It's Timmins. They're all trying to get us in that mine. Us. You and me. And Pop. After all, he found the horseshoes."

Mattie added, "And he got me here."

So all that was left now was to go into the tunnel and see what this was all about. That conclusion did not need to be spoken, was not welcome. My head felt like a pinball machine: one small silver ball trying to hit the one right pin.

"Let's not go to the mine tonight." I was practically pleading.

Mattie seemed ready to go, but she gave in easily. My relief disappeared quickly, however, as I recognized Turrell's dark figure on the porch outside the open window near our table. He had been drinking a bottle of beer, slouched in a chair, and as he stood up he filled the window with his menacing frame. He waited until he caught my eye before he disappeared into the deepness of the night.

Pop didn't see him; Mattie did. Pop watched us as we pushed ourselves back from the table. "Who's hungry?" I asked.

That night grew into one of separation from Pop and seclusion with Mattie. Around my house, the singing insects raised their voices. We were angry with Pop's brain for stashing so many secrets and with his spirit for failing to retrieve them. Inside, on the living room floor, bunching up the rug as our bodies found their fit, we went into our own mine, our own cavern, and didn't come out until an early ray of morning sun found our eyelashes.

23

A morning of promise and of fear, bright blue above and dry and dusty below, brought the mountains too close to the eyes. I wondered how Janice was doing. Celita would know. I wondered what would become of Janice. Maybe nothing. Maybe nothing at all. And I wished something terrible would become of Turrell. If I were a person who could give curses, I would curse Turrell. Turn him into a dead weed.

I walked down to the cafe, arriving before Celita or Baby. Mattie had gone down ahead of me to the hotel to get Pop going. The day did not feel right, like a piece was missing, a jagged hole in a jigsaw puzzle scene. I sat at the counter, my back to the morning, a little anxious. Unsettled. Suddenly the door flew open and Mattie came straight for me, taking both my arms in her firm hands. Her face was tightened around her eyes and mouth. "You can't get upset. I mean, we need to talk—Pop is gone. He's missing. And he's not at the mine. I don't know where he is. Carla never saw him leave the hotel. No one in the dining room saw him. I don't think he even slept in his bed. He's just gone."

I stared at her as she talked, my mouth open, stunned. "Wait a minute," I said when my voice found me. "Wait a minute, no one has seen him? Tell me everything again." I was shaking. We sat down at a table, and I held Mattie's hands. She told me she'd gone into his room when he hadn't answered the door. It looked like he hadn't slept in his bed. She ran down to talk to Carla, who had been there early, since six-thirty, and had not seen him come down. John was preparing breakfast in the hotel kitchen and said he didn't see Pop come in the dining room. None of the waitresses had seen him either. The bar wasn't open. He wasn't in any of the bathrooms. Mattie drove to the mine to find a crude *Closed Today for Repairs* sign on the gate. She called the sheriff, who said his deputy would keep an eye out for Pop.

I was quiet when she finished her story. All I could think of was Turrell standing outside the window in the bar the night before. "Turrell's got him."

Mattie looked surprised. "What?"

"It's Turrell." I got up from the table and walked around the cafe. "He's got something to do with this. Let's call the sheriff and tell him about Turrell—"

"Tell him what?" Mattie followed my agitated pacing. "There's nothing we can tell him."

She was right. What proof did we have that Turrell was after Pop? But I knew he had Pop. Turning abruptly into her face I said, "You said the mine was closed? That's pretty weird. Did you go to Elmo's? He probably closed the mine so he could drink all day."

"It's not open yet." Mattie was patient with my wild search for truth.

"I wish I knew where he lived. Maybe Janice knows. We need to find Turrell." I kept thinking of the mine being closed. "Let's go to the mine."

She tried to keep up with me, but her composure was slipping.

"But it's closed! Kate, it's closed. He's not there." Her eyes filled up with premature sorrow. "Maybe Randall came and took him back to Tombstone in the middle of the night."

"Come on." Randall did not have him. Turrell did.

White sunlight stretched as far as it could into the mine, laying the shadow of the chain-link gate like a tattered rug on the ground. I couldn't see the train.

"Let's use the key and go in." Now Mattie was brave.

"Wait. Pop can't be in there unless Turrell is. I don't want him to know about the key."

"The train's not there." She looked at me, perplexed. "What's he repairing? Maybe he took the train into the tunnel to repair something further in. Maybe a rail. Do you think Pop's in there?"

We were whispering now. "I don't know."

I was torn between risking our secret key to look for Pop and accepting the more mundane, anticlimactic fact that Randall retrieved Pop in the middle of the night. But what good was the key anyway if Pop was back in Tombstone? What good was the mine, what good were the matchmaking ghosts? Maybe the mule came and took Pop away while we were sleeping. Maybe the man on the mule in the dreams wasn't Blue after all, but Pop. I reached deep into Mattie's eyes and felt the darkness, the low, vibrating hum.

My fingers found the warm key deep inside my pocket, and as it traveled from darkness into light, our hearts raced. So discreet, so stupid, so desperate to find our lost friend. We didn't have a flashlight. And we couldn't turn on the lights and give away our presence. So we walked until gray became pitch black, and then we stood still and listened. All we heard was a muted clanking sound every now and then—no voices, no screams, no gunshots. We waited for what seemed like an hour. Holding onto each other, we made our way back toward the light of day. Just as we got to the shadow of the gate, a rumbling sound flew toward us from behind, and as we turned to look, a big ball of swirling dust rushed through us and out into the hot, sunlit air. Coughing and frantically unlocking the gate with blinking eyes, we rushed out behind the dust and threw ourselves into the jeep, rocking it with our gasping. Our hands tried to soothe our eyes.

Mattie spoke first. "What happened? What the hell happened?" She looked toward the gate. "Was it the train? What—" She slowly turned and looked at me, stinging tears from her dusty eyes leaving trails in the powdery layer on her skin. "It was that ghost, wasn't it? It was that goddamn ghost."

"Yeah," I said, as I wiped the dust off my face with the bottom of my T-shirt, "just like the story, just like Francisco said."

We sat there, sweating in the heat of a black jeep baking in the sun. Two cigarettes calmed Mattie, and the frequent cars passing by on the road helped bring me back to reality, or something. Helped me regain rhythmic breathing, helped slow my heart.

"OK. Now what are we going to do? We have to find Pop." Mattie was starting over. I was hungry.

Back at the cafe, dirty and gathering stares, we ate as if there would be no food tomorrow. Celita watched us as she worked, waiting for what we needed. Finally she came over to our table.

"Where's Pop? Why are you so dirty? Where have you been? Where's Pop?"

I looked up at her loving, angry face. "Celita, you worry too much. Nothing is wrong. I want you to do something for me." I finished my soda, and as I stood up I could see she did not believe me. "Come here." Taking her arm, I walked her out the back door. The cicadas gave us a startled hello.

"All right. We don't know where Pop is. The sheriff's keeping an eye out for him. He's not at the mine. Well, I don't think he is." A big sigh reinforced my words. "Listen, do you know where Turrell lives?"

Her eyes said at once that I was crazy and that she was upset. "Mr. Randall must've come and taken him back! Call him. Call Mr. Randall."

"OK, I will." I wouldn't call Randall. Not yet. "So do you know where Turrell lives?"

"No." Now she looked confused. "Why?"

I opened the door and took us back in the cafe. "Why? Who knows? I don't know, I don't know why!" My voice was getting louder, and I guess Celita had had enough of me. She went behind the counter and resumed her cooking as I stood there in front of the bathroom door. I smelled cigarette smoke and yanked the unlocked door open to find Baby blowing smoke out the window. I pointed my furious finger at her and said over and over again as she slid past me out to the customers, "That's it! That's it!" I didn't know what I meant, but I knew it had nothing to do with Baby or her cigarette smoke.

I saw Mattie's hand up in the air waving at me, pointing to her empty glass. She wanted another Coke. I wanted to know where Turrell lived. I wanted to go over there with my imaginary double-barreled shotgun and rescue Pop. Maybe he was at St. Elmo's now.

Plopping Mattie's Coke down in front of her, I announced, "I'm going to Elmo's to see if Turrell is in there." As I stepped onto the sidewalk I heard her push her chair away from the table and the heels of her boots made their way heavily to my side.

At Elmo's, smoke and rotten beer tried to keep us out of the searing darkness, but we stepped in despite it all. Red-rimmed eyes floated in the darkness. Grumbling sounds rose to the ceiling, and the hard sound of the pool balls smacked the thick air. Turrell wasn't there. Neither was Pop.

The blue air outside pulled us back into the light. Time to try Janice.

The phone rang twenty-three times before I gave up. I pictured Janice passed out at the kitchen table while the phone yawned its rings one by one.

"Celita, have you talked to Janice today?"

"No." She was not happy with me.

Mattie had an idea.

"Listen. One of us can call Elmo's and ask for him, pretending to be his sister or some other relative. We can ask them for his address—tell them its an emergency, that we're in town and need to get to him."

"Or get someone to call pretending to be Billy Beecham needing him for an emergency at the mine, can't remember where he lives, once he finds out Turrell's not at Elmo's he'll need to try to get him at his home." Who would pretend to be Billy? I thought John might do it.

"They'll probably just give us his phone number, not his address." Mattie was right.

I tried the phone book, but Turrell Fisher didn't really exist. We called the sheriff, to be told there had been no sign of Pop.

Mattie led me to the door. "Let's go to the hotel, then up to your house, see if he's there. Maybe he—" She stopped abruptly. "The cemetery! We didn't check the cemetery!" We ran full speed toward the jeep. Why didn't I think of that? Of course that's where he was.

He wasn't. He wasn't bent over Jack Timmins' tombstone. He wasn't wandering through marble and mesquite. His wiry frame wasn't stirring in the breeze with the thin, worn, hanging rosaries. He wasn't there. He was somewhere with Turrell. We went back to the hotel, deflated and silent.

Carla saw us dragging by on our way upstairs. She gave us a pitying look and didn't say a word, so we knew Pop's room would be empty. No sign of him in his room or Mattie's. I missed my rage. Pulling an empty, defeated frame around did not suit me.

My house didn't have Pop either. Just a whistling breeze playing in the mesquite leaves over the little bird grave.

We drove to the post office, the bank, every store, and back to the mine. Absolutely nothing had changed. We drove to Janice's and killed her doorbell. Then we found ourselves at Beecham's Hardware Store. Nothing mattered anymore but finding Pop. We walked inside, through narrow disheveled aisles and big wooden bins full of nails. A man with a face the shape and color of a raw tomato asked us if he could help us. Billy Beecham and his family were out of town for a few days, and Turrell Fisher was not a familiar name to the man or to his coworker. The Twilight Zone. None of this existed. Mattie and I were beings hailing from another plane of existence, another reality, fantasizing about what it would be like to be human living on the earth. We weren't doing a very good job.

We drove back to my house. I stopped on the porch and asked the grand-prize blue ribbon mule shoes where Pop was. They hung in stillness on their nails, saying nothing. They knew, I know they did. I saw over the hills that dusk was close by. I could not bear nightfall without knowing what had happened to Pop. Nightfall would finish it. Missing people were never found. If someone did not come home for the whole day, they never would. To ward off the fall of night, my rage came creeping back.

Mattie was sitting on the floor talking on the phone when I walked in the house. I hoped it wasn't to Randall. She looked up at me as she hung up. "I was just checking in at home, talking to my brother to see if everything was OK."

I nodded. "Is it?" I felt rage tightening my frame, my features, my voice. I missed the fact that it was odd for her to be calling home at this particular time.

"Yes, it is." She got up, stood close in front of me, and caressed my face in her hands. "I'm going to run to the store and get us some ice cream. Then we'll talk about calling Randall. Don't call him. I'll be right back."

I sat on the edge of the couch and stared at the living room in general. Tightened, denying the settling darkness, I stared at the stilled phone on the floor. After what felt like a long time, the phone startled me with a ring. I picked it up to hear Mattie's slightly higher voice. "Kate, get your car, Turrell's at Elmo's and I've—" That was enough. I was in my car and hurtling down the road. I slammed into the curb in front of Turrell standing on the sidewalk. He flinched as the car door slammed behind me. I backed him up against the building with my momentum.

"Where the hell is Pop, you shitface! You tell me where he is or I'm going to murder you!" Suddenly Mattie's hand was firmly on my shoulder, but not firmly enough. I couldn't stand the moment. I couldn't stand his narrowed hateful eyes telling me to get away from him. I couldn't stand the scream coming out of my mouth, the tears blurting out of my eyes. I was lost in a rage in my own town, on my own sidewalk. I heard a new sound in my head, a crisp, clean click as my right arm rose up in a surprised flying fist. I felt my knuckles push back into my wrist as I connected with Turrell's rib cage. He slid down onto the sidewalk and slumped over. Mattie pushed me into my car, jumped into the driver's seat, and peeled out, leaving a streetlamp in the rearview mirror to look down on Turrell's still, deflated shape on the sidewalk.

"Goddamn it! Shit, Kate!" Her hands gripped the steering wheel in a death hold. "Shit!"

Tears were gushing down my face, and I couldn't move my hand. I was afraid to look at it, the smoking shotgun. Powder burns. My hand would die. I sobbed for it.

Mattie slammed on the brakes in front of the cafe, ran in, came out dragging Pop behind her, and practically threw him in the back seat. Through my wet eyes I saw him there, stiff against the seat back, a pale apparition.

"Matt, take me to the hospital." I turned my precarious attention to my smoking hand.

"I am." The car sped past the mine, leaving Bisbee behind for the little one-story hospital just past the gaping, dark Flagg Pit.

The long white curtain pulled around my cubicle in the emergency room showed the moving, protruding shape of a doctor as she maneuvered around my neighbor in the tight quarters. She told the coughing man to breathe slowly into the mask. I wanted a mask. I wanted Mattie to talk. She wouldn't say anything. I asked her to shoot my hand. She wouldn't say anything. Later she told me she was worrying that the next patient in would be Turrell and she couldn't handle that scene.

"OK. I've got the X-rays. It's not broken. Bruised knucklebones and a sprain. Let's wrap it up for a couple of days. You go easy on it. No more slugfests, missy. I'll give you some painkillers. You're lucky it's not broken. You'll be all right." The doctor was all right. I wasn't. I started crying again. Mattie rubbed my back softly with the palm of her hand as a nurse wrapped an ugly Ace bandage around my spent, limp fist.

As we drove back to the hotel, Mattie told me her sneaky story.

She had called St. Elmo's, not her brother, from my house while I was on the porch trying to get information from the horseshoes. Turrell was there, with an old man. She thought if she told me, or brought me with her, something like just what happened would happen. She went in there with the intention of ignoring Turrell and taking Pop out and up to my house. She didn't have to ignore him. When she walked in she saw Pop sitting at the bar. Turrell was shooting pool, his back to Mattie. She walked up to Pop, grasped his arm firmly, took the whiskey glass out of his hand, and set it softly on the bar. He went with her easily, and no one seemed to notice, or maybe they knew he belonged with Mattie.

They walked out onto the sidewalk to the jeep. Mattie bounced into the driver's seat, ready to rip out of there with her treasure, only to face another obstacle. The jeep wouldn't start. It tried, but just couldn't do it. She took Pop quickly into the cafe and sat him away from the window. With cool, deadly six-gun eyes, she told him, "You leave this cafe and I'll hunt you down, no matter how long it takes. And when I find you, I'll skin you alive and hang your hide in my living room." She called me from the phone in the cafe. My response sent her out onto the sidewalk to catch the whirling dust devil coming down the canyon. When she saw me flying at Turrell, who had just come out of the bar, her boots made the fastest start of their lives. But not fast enough to prevent the outlaw fist's rocket to the ribs.

24

Pop didn't speak for three days. Although my hand felt better, I was afraid to leave the house. I knew Turrell would be waiting, lurking at every street corner, to murder me. I was frozen in time, in terror, unable to imagine what the rest of my life could be. John charged the battery and got the jeep started. Mattie scooted back and forth between the hotel, the cafe, and my house, impatient and flustered. None of her reports soothed me. And her theory of what happened, Pop's kidnapping, fell on closed ears.

"Turrell didn't go to the hospital. He's probably lying up at his house drunk, not knowing his ribs are busted. Maybe he'll die." In my silence, she talked on and on.

"This is what I think. Turrell took Pop out of the hotel in the middle of the night and took him to the mine to force him to show him that damn treasure he thinks is buried there. Why else would he take Pop? I mean, with all his snooping around, he must think there's money involved. So he puts up that *Closed Today for Repairs* sign. I hope he didn't hurt Pop, but who knows? Pop hasn't uttered the tiniest clue, nothing. Won't say a word. Oh my God! The ghost, Timmins' ghost! Pop was probably in there when that happened to us." She had jumped up from her seat on the edge of the couch, and the cushions rose under me at the sudden absence of her sweet weight. Turning around toward my slumped shape, she expected as much excitement from me at the thought of Blue appearing to Pop in the mine. I wouldn't budge.

"God, Kate." She came over to me and melted her body around mine, caving in to her worry. "Please come back."

We sat in that warmth on the couch for a long time, and I felt the safety of her words. "Turrell won't hurt you. Everyone thinks you gave him what he deserved. No one's going to let him hurt you. It's OK." She pulled away enough to look into my eyes to tell me what I needed to hear. "I love you for what you did, it just scared me to death. But now I think I know what happened to you, and you're still here, and so am I." She kissed me. "Please come back to me. I can't stand this."

My three days of grief and terror flew slowly away on whispering wings. Mattie knew that I had horrified myself with my slugging fist, that I mourned the part of myself that would never think to hit someone. That the weapon should be punished. That revenge was waiting to take my life. And that I had been alone with all this. I left the house with her, checked my horseshoes and Koko's grave, smelled the heat, breathed the high air. There was Bisbee, still mine. I had a sense that it was mine even more now. I held onto her tightly as we walked down to the cafe.

Pop ended his silence when I came back. He began mumbling about Blue and his gun and where was his horse. There was a different look to his face. It seemed tighter, his eyes narrower, as if he were trying to keep something from seeping out.

I had a new nickname, and Mattie wouldn't smile about it until I did. John Belton started it because he was so delighted with my changed status: Calamity Kate. Bisbee now had a hero who had kicked up the dust of so many dead fantasies.

The cafe was airy and humming. "It's about time." Celita had tried to come see me, when I wouldn't see anyone, after my crime. Now she was mad, relieved, and happy at the same time. Baby ignored me and busied herself, and all the customers smiled at me in unison.

Mattie and I sat at the table with Pop and Francisco, who was back to his daily routine after his mysterious absence. His eyes seemed livelier, brighter. I knew what was happening. What I had seen as an act of shameful violence was really a collective psychic taking-back for Bisbee what the town was fundamentally about. Bisbee was a ghost mine, a humming cemetery, a beautiful stirring soul reaching up to the bluest of skies. Dancing stories, bouncing laughter, people walking arm in arm on the wooden sidewalks into the wee hours of the starriest nights. I guess I felt the victory then, and knew it completely. I never worried about Turrell again.

25

Temporarily Closed. The sign was brand new, its red paint still sticky. Calamity Kate had closed the mine. No more train tours. We supposed Billy would search for a new tour operator, not wanting to muddy his image with a drunken, street-brawling loser of an employee. So the Copper Queen yawned in front of us, ready for some action.

"We'll be back tonight," I said to the wide-open mouth, and Mattie put her arm around my shoulders. We stood there looking into the darkness, seeing all the bright possibilities offered now. The afternoon was still, few cars sped by on the highway, and the parking lot was empty. A couple of crows flew in the sky south of us, just about where the big pit was. Looking behind me at Bisbee's rooftops, I could see the hotel standing on its tiptoes to keep sight of us.

The sound of grinding tires under the big, long Oldsmobile as it turned onto the pavement interrupted my sense of psychic order. It was Janice. The heavy door defied her feeble attempt to gently push it shut. She was drunk.

"Well, look there." She sauntered up to us, holding her purse in one hand as its shoulder strap dragged on the ground. "The mad desperado and her cute little angel. I would've shot his ugly face off." She laughed like a hyena and tripped on her purse strap. Righting her steps just before she reached us, she changed her tune. "I've been lookin' for you two. Any luck with the mine?"

I ignored her question. "Janice, you want to come up to the

house and visit Koko's grave?" I thought she needed that instead of what she had now.

"No. No!" She turned awkwardly from us and wove the few feet to the mine entrance. "Billy's little hellhole. I swear that son of a bitch was born in there."

Mattie went up to Janice. I didn't know what she thought she was going to accomplish with gentle enticement, which was what I expected from her. But that's not what she did. Her voice was firm, shaking, her eyes deeply serious as she and Janice faced off. "I'd get you another bird if I thought you could take care of it." The five inches between their faces shimmered. Janice backed away, her eyes on Mattie's tight mouth, all the way to her car. It took her three tries to get the door shut, and the tires grunted as they carried her and her heavy life back down the road to Lowell.

"Pop won't go in the mine tonight." Mattie put a bag of groceries down on the kitchen counter and turned on the lights. The phone rang, and I turned away from my dusk watch at the window to answer it, repeating Mattie's words in my head. It was Thea.

"Hey, girl! Miss Calamity Kate! That's one up on Cactus Kate, wouldn't you say? Well, you are quite something. Making the streets of Bisbee safer for us all. I know a creep up my street I should point you toward. I just had to call and congratulate you. Marta says you should be sheriff—Calamity Kate, Sheriff of Cochise County. I think it's a damn good idea!"

"Yeah. I'm making up campaign posters right now." I looked at Mattie thrashing in the grocery bag. "Thea, I can't talk now. I'll call you back later, OK? Your vote of confidence has touched my heart. And, please, thank Marta for me."

I went quietly into the kitchen to wait for some explanation. Mattie found what she was looking for at the bottom of the bag. Flashlight batteries. She threw them onto the counter amid the lettuce, pears, pasta, and Pepsi, and dropped down into a chair at the table. She lit a cigarette. A feisty face spit out her dismay. "After all this time—'get me in there, get the horses, get the guns'—now he won't go. Now he's scared to death of that mine. That goddamn Turrell—"

"It's not Turrell." I knew. "It's Blue. It's the grave. It's that raging cloud of dust." I put my hand under her chin and tilted her sweet hurt face up to mine. "Let's talk to him."

"How? How can we talk to Pop? Just how *do* we talk to him?"

"It's worth a try, don't you think?" I wasn't sure of that, actually. Maybe we'd just drag him in there against his will. Giving up the plan altogether was not an option.

Mattie smashed her cigarette in the rusted tin can bottom I found just for her, and blew her words out with the last stream of smoke. "Sometimes I wish my relationship with Pop was simply a matter of who was the fastest draw, out in the street, the two of us at high noon with the whole town watching." The cigarette butt was quite dead.

I reminded her, "We'll talk to him tomorrow. Let's eat."

She threw me a funny look. "I left him in the hotel bar. He won't go up to his room until the bar closes." She was annoyed. "Guess he's afraid of everything now." In a nighttime greeting, she went to the window and looked out at Koko's grave, holding a hand up to the glass. She did that a lot.

Later, over steaming pasta, I asked her what had happened to her with Janice earlier in the day. She took a while to answer. "I don't know, I guess I just can't stand seeing her drunk anymore. Can't help her, and I can't hurt her. She's got a crazed heart."

"I think you can hurt her."

"You think I hurt her feelings today? I think I just made her mad."

"Same thing, really."

She poked at the pasta remnants with her fork. "It's so weird, though. We have her damn bird buried here, and she's riding around drunk harrassing us."

It *was* weird. But it was Janice. "I'm sorry." I pushed my chair back from the table. "She's a pain in the ass. You know, though, there's something about her."

Mattie joined me at the sink. Over the clatter of dishes and the rushing water she said with finality, "The 'something about her' is just my stupid expectations."

"I remember you expected her to transform into a prophet or something."

"Well, maybe not."

We plunked down in front of the TV and flipped ourselves through the channels to sleep.

I sat across from Pop, oblivious to the rest of the cafe, watching his sleepy face grind into its tight hold. His morning coffee sent its steam up to try to soften, smooth over, the battleground. I thought of his notes. Of his pleas, his demands of Elizabeth. If only he knew she was following us around. Maybe, I thought, he was seeing her, too. Maybe she was coming to him in his room, maybe he saw her in the mine. I wanted to tell Mattie, but I left her to her morning banter with Celita over the counter. We had agreed I would attempt to talk with Pop about the mine because Mattie was too annoyed with him to have any luck. She would say too much, feed the fear.

He stared at the steam, looking through me, through the building across the street, through the hills behind it.

Nothing more to wait for. Maybe the sound of my voice would come to him from inside those hills, more important, more impressive than where he'd gone. "I know where Wyatt is. I know where he's trapped. I snuck in when it was dark, and I saw him. We can get him, I figured it out. They'll never see us. But we'll have to leave the horses in the rocks, go in on foot. Elizabeth will wait with the horses, keep them quiet. You and me and Mattie will go in and get him."

His eyes were focused on me now, unsquinted and liquid. I had him.

I lowered my voice and leaned across the table toward him. "Wyatt looked thin. We better go in as soon as possible, I think tonight, don't want to waste any time."

That was enough. I put my finger to my closed lips to seal our secret plan. Pop began to mumble about his horse, his gun. He was back. Turrell was gone. Just Pop's original, pure adventure remained. Tonight was the night. I leaned back in my chair and let out a soft sigh of relief. I couldn't let Pop leave this world fearful and closed up. I wanted him to go out with his pal Wyatt Earp riding behind him on his horse, kicking up getaway dust on their way into the Mule Mountains.

26

"Should we be doing this? Wyatt Earp is *not* in that mine—only the ghost of someone who knew Pop." Mattie had on a yellow hard hat with a lamp on the front. She looked great, checking herself out in my mirror.

"What are you talking about?" I joined her at the mirror with my hard hat. Somehow I wasn't as stunning in it as she was. "Just remember that Elizabeth wants us in that mine. How can you forget that?" I adjusted the hat for a better look.

"Yeah."

She took off the hat and stuck it in the big canvas bag with four flashlights, spare batteries, a pack, a water bottle, a battery-powered lantern, and four apples. I had asked her why four apples and she said dryly, "One for Mr. Earp."

I thought of the horseshoes up on the porch. "Do you think we should take the mule its other shoes?" Suddenly it seemed that we both were struck with the gravity of what we were about to do. The silence was made out of steel, our eyes locking hands, our hearts remembering the first moment we saw each other, our bodies remembering the mine, the creek in the canyon, the water, the jolt.

We stood facing each other in a familiar trance. Mattie moved effortlessly through the gravity and removed my yellow hard hat with the lamp in front and kissed me. I know she kissed me because all the stars in the sky appeared in an instant on my bedroom ceiling. With no more words, we threw the canvas bag into the jeep and drove down the canyon to pick up Pop at the hotel. I chuckled at the thought of Pop in a yellow hard hat.

The jeep rolled quietly to a stop in front of the hotel. We sat staring at the big, silent witness to the hidden days of copper ore, flowing whiskey, struggling mules, and tragic miners. The twilight was giving way to a full yellow moon. Just a few people sat on the big porch of the Copper Queen Hotel.

Mattie's little bit of doubt persisted. "I wonder if he can really walk that far in the dark with a flashlight. Maybe he's not strong enough."

I turned to look at her and said slowly, finally, "He's strong enough." With that we were out of the jeep and into the hotel. Carla was picking her teeth with a strong-smelling mint toothpick. "Pop's in the bar," she announced. I went in and found him sitting on his stool, finishing a glass of whiskey. My timing was perfect. I touched his shoulder and spoke softly into his ear as he turned his face toward me. "We're going in. It's time." Standing back, I waited for him to put his hat on and nod good night to the bartender. He followed me out, and Mattie took up behind us as our sneaky parade left through the hotel doors. He never said a word, but his face was perked like a dog's sniffing something good on the wind.

We parked the jeep in our usual spot at the far end of the parking lot away from the streetlamp near the mine entrance. With the first lull in passing traffic, Pop between us, we went straight for the gate and were in quickly. I put the canvas bag down in the dirt and looked at Pop. His eyes were bigger and his mouth was tightening. I took his hat off and tried to put the yellow hard hat on his head, but he would have nothing to do with it. We scuffled in the dust for a few seconds until I gave up. I looked at Mattie for some help, and her thoughtful face proclaimed a fair decision. "Well, none of us will wear them. If we do, Wyatt may not recognize us."

Of course, how stupid of us.

I put everything in the pack except the discarded hats, and Mattie and I got on either side of Pop, each locking an arm around an arm. We walked slowly, following our flashlights' spread-out beams, alongside the rails, past the train as it rested silently, promising to keep our secret, matching our stride with Pop's small, quick steps. His breathing was shallow, rapid like a bird's. The only sound was the crunching of six boot heels in the rocky dirt as we moved deeper into the tunnel.

The thin, black air rushed through my teeth, filling my demanding lungs.

"I think it's time for a rest," Mattie proclaimed in a high, strained voice. No sooner were the words out of her mouth than Pop stopped abruptly. We rested right there.

"Anyone want an apple?" Mattie sounded nervous now.

"Maybe later." I moved the light around the spot where we stood, hoping to see some congratulatory sign from Elizabeth. Nothing but a few little rusted pieces of metal denting the dirt, and rocks. Above us the timbering looked solid; I wanted to trust that we really didn't need those hard hats. Pop began mumbling and I threw my flashlight beam in his face. His eyes were shrinking into their wild, darting stance. I worried that he would bolt for the gate. Instead, he put a scrawny finger to my face and muttered something about Elizabeth. Had he seen her? Had he felt her there? He started walking, and we scrambled to fall in line with him with our flashlights. He was headed further into the tunnel, as if he knew where he was going, stumbling slightly on the many little rocks, but persisting. Mattie and I glanced at each other behind his head in an attempt to remind each other that we wanted to be here.

We got to the entrance to the first tunnel and were greeted by a couple of bats flapping frantically above our heads. Mattie and I jumped ahead, but Pop seemed oblivious to the intrusion. So, steady on, we reached the second tunnel before stopping for another rest, drinking a little water in silence. No muttering, no conversation. Mattie's eyes met mine in a constant game of tag. Pop's breathing was audible now under the physical strain, but not labored. We moved into the tunnel and paused at the cavern, the carved-out horseshoe, the scenic viewpoint. The pause was long enough for Pop to notice something in the dirt and bend over to pick it up. As he straightened up with his find, my heart knocked once loudly. Pop wiped off that hat we had found before, fixed its shape as best he could, and turned to Mattie.

She was frozen, her eyes stuck to the hat. Pop reached up and put it on Mattie's head. I started crying. A perfect fit, and she looked right as rain in that hat. The moment cracked in two as some rocky dirt, a little crumble of ceiling, let go and landed at our feet. We all jumped at once. My tears made way for a pounding heart and a reassuring voice. "It's OK, see, there's no more. It happens all the time, just a little gentle shifting. Everything's fine." Mattie's flashlight scanned the world above us and crossed paths with mine.

"Yeah," she said, "it's OK. Let's keep going." She checked Pop, who had not lost his momentum. Mattie seemed relaxed now, fearless in her new hat, as if she'd worn it all her life. I took her hand as Pop walked a foot in front of us. We pointed our lights just ahead of him, illuminating the ground as it passed by his dusty boots.

The warmth jumping around between our clinched hands pulled Mattie and me further into the darkness, further into trust. We were moving toward something, and every moment existing before this one ripped by me, a gusty wind blowing Pop further on.

"This is a dream," whispered Mattie. "This is a dream hat." Her eyes loomed large and moist above the far-reaching flashlights' rays. "Are you OK?" The tunnel narrowed.

I didn't know what she meant, so I didn't answer her. I watched the back of Pop's adventure. His drooping shoulders, his sagging pants seat, his white hair falling from under his hat and covering the back of his neck. My heart was crazy. Our steps in the dirt grew louder until they sounded more like hooves. *Here we go. It's mule time.* I began to hear the distant metallic sounds, and the air smelled like hide. My whole body buzzed. I ruined Mattie's dreaming.

"Can you hear those sounds—the mules' hooves, the clanking?" I stopped us as I spoke. Pop kept going. Mattie's face showed me her disappointment. This wasn't a dream, and now I was going to get weird. She gathered my face in her hands, searched my eyes, said "No." We both sighed and let our heads rest together, forehead to forehead. When we turned into the light beams to continue on, Pop was not there. We quickened our pace, bathing the walls on either side with light, but the tunnel was too narrow for him to be unseen against the walls. We moved straight ahead into the galloping lights, fighting panic. I tightened my brain to make the sounds and smells leave, to make room for this terror, this task. He had disappeared. Poof. Gone. Again. We found him each time before. We would find him now.

"He can only be just a little ahead of us. Don't worry. The worst thing that could happen is that he'll fall and break something and we can carry him back and—"

Mattie's scream interrupted. "Pop! Pop!"

I joined in. "Pop! Hold up, wait for us! Wait for the light! Wait up!"

"Pop, wait!"

Our screams scattered the bats and bounced off the rock walls like a million ping-pong balls. We stopped screaming for him then, and everything settled down. Walking quickly, our steps were taut, frightened. The tunnel widened. The hooves hit the dirt steadily in my head, and the clanging of metal grew louder. Where the hell was he? The darkness surrounding our meager light beam grew thicker, oppressive. This was not a twilight, not like my dusks that let me sit in them while they slowly sank deeper and deeper into darkness. I wanted my mother to turn on the light. I squeezed my eyes shut and saw her turning on the lights in every room of our small, square, humid house. "There," she would say, "you're a crazy kid."

When I opened my eyes I noticed the train rails began breaking up. Crooked, escaping sections lay in the dirt. Had Pop tripped over them? How could he keep going in the dark? The tracks ended in a mess of steel debris. A little further ahead the tunnel ended, widening into a circular stage. The sounds in my head ended. Our flashlights found Pop sitting on a big rock, his hands gripping it on each side of his skinny seat. He was muttering and turning his head back and forth. He didn't even look at us as we approached him.

He was in another world. Mattie sat next to him on the edge of the rock, her back to his shoulder, and took out the water bottle. She drank, then shoved the bottle into his arm. He ignored it. I took the bottle, feeling the cool stream of water break apart the tight cords of fear in my chest. Mattie put the four flashlights in the dirt pointing up, in various positions around us, and hung the lantern from a rusted bolt in a beam above us. Our end of the road brightened. I looked down. All around, in the dirt in front of Pop's feet, were hoofprints.

Old or new, I guess it didn't matter. And there were a few footprints, obviously ours. I wondered if the mule had appeared to Pop, dancing in front of him as he sat on the rock, telling him a thing or two. Would a spirit leave hoofprints? If a spirit could leave its shoes, or its hat, yes. The air seemed different in this rounded end of the road. Stubborn, evasive. Mattie went to light a cigarette, then changed her mind.

We both scanned with discerning eyes this place where Blue Timmins had been murdered. Shot to death, a long time ago. Rock walls and ceiling, dirt floor, posts and beams holding it all up. Nothing different about this tunnel, except the air.

The silence was overwhelming. Pop had stopped muttering and was staring straight ahead. Mattie got up and stood in front of him, hands on hips, and spoke to him. "OK, buddy," she demanded. "What do we do now?"

He looked at her with the clearest eyes I'd seen on him, and said calmly, "He's dead."

"Yeah, I'm sorry. It looks that way." Mattie relaxed her stance. "Are you OK?"

Mattie and I saw her at the same time. Lizzy was standing behind Pop, holding the big rock he was sitting on in her hands, but he was still sitting on the rock in front of her. She was gone in a second. As Pop was saying, "Where did that horse go?" Mattie asked him to get off the rock. He moved stiffly, sitting on a bigger rock that jutted out from the wall of long-hidden copper ore.

"Help me push it over." We got on our knees and pushed as hard as we could until the rock tipped over. We sat in the dirt staring at an old, narrow, flat leather book. Mattie picked it up and brushed it off, looked at me with serious, excited eyes, and opened it. Inside were some papers, yellowed but intact. The first was a flyer about the opera in Tombstone. The second was an old certificate for a mining claim in Pop's name. We looked at each other, then back at Pop sitting against the rock wall. "Kate, remember I told you about someone in Tombstone hearing that Pop lost a mining claim to someone a long time ago? Maybe it was Timmins. Maybe Pop found Timmins in Bisbee, saw him in some saloon or something and recognized him—"

"Are you saying that Pop killed Timmins?" I whispered as she looked back down at the claim.

"To get the claim back."

I knew this. Because someone or something was showing it to me in my head. Timmins put that book under the rock. Pop drew his gun and ducked as Timmins threw a pick ax at him, shooting several bullets and killing Jack "Blue" Timmins. The only witness was a pack mule. Pop rode the mule out of the mine. I could see it all. And the familiar images came to me from my dreams—a man on a mule. It had been Pop. And the mule falling through the sky. And the horseshoes. I tried to tell Mattie quickly, in a low voice. I'm not sure if she got it all or was too stunned to respond, but she stood up and said,

"Let's give this back to Pop."

We went over to where he sat and knelt beside him. I couldn't see his face under the shadow of his hat, but he seemed at ease. Mattie held out the book. "Here, Pop. You came here to get this back, didn't you? Here it is. It's yours now."

I thought about the other story, that Pop had ridden with Wyatt Earp, his hero. Pop, the famous would-be gunfighter full of fantastic stories, who finally killed someone here deep in the mine. He had been tormented ever since. He wasn't really a gunfighter. Didn't have it in him. Pop was a poor prospector, a kid, wandering the desert mountains on his horse in search of glistening silver. He had left Wyatt, the gunfighter, in this tunnel, and the torment had brought him back.

"Here. Don't you want this?" Mattie touched the book to his hand resting on his knee. He wasn't budging. I leaned closer and looked up under his hat at his face. His eyes had the same clarity, his face changed to a new smooth and peaceful look. I put my hand on his knotty knuckles and the sunken skin around them, and I knew that he was dead. My heart pounded to escape as I turned to Mattie, who stood up quickly from her kneeling position. She knew. She took her hat off, and holding it in her hand, hitting it gently against her thigh, she walked around the eerily lit space, stirring the dust as Pop's death hadn't. I sat limply in the dirt at Pop's feet, hearing her cry. Should I feel for a pulse? Could we breathe and pound life back into him? But he was gone. I had felt it in his still, wooden hand. He had died when we found his claim. The air collapsed in my chest.

A loud sound came quickly, penetrating the tunnel, the dead body, my soul and Mattie's. It was the other-worldly cry of a mule, full force, thrown purposefully through our skin. Pop's body shifted downward; his head slumped forward but his hat stayed on. The thunder of hooves descended on us through a funnel of dust, sped out of the tunnel, and was gone. And so was Pop's spirit.

Mattie and I grabbed each other and held on for dear life, trying to breathe, scared to death, exhilarated. As the dust settled, so did we. We gradually unfolded from each other, coughed away dying dust, and turned to look at the dead demented gunfighter. His black-clad bones left perched on a rock a mile back in a forgotten tunnel of the Copper Queen.

Leaning my shoulder into the rock wall of this new double tomb, I imagined Pop's body now as rock. An old, crumbly rock. I looked down at his body, at the back of his head, the brim of his hat. His hair stirred slightly in the little swirls of air left by the mule's departure. Mattie stood some distance away, her arms tight across her chest, her head bowed down as her boots took her in little zigzag lines in the dirt. She was crying again. I talked to the back of Pop's head.

"What do we do now? You want to stay in here? What do we do?" My tears came one by one. "We can't leave without you. What am I going to tell Celita?" I saw the leather book lying in the dirt where Mattie had dropped it. A corner of it touched the toe of one of Pop's boots. I bent down and picked it up. It fit smoothly into a back pocket of my jeans. A heaviness sat me down again in front of Pop's boots, his thin legs, his hand clawlike around a knee. Mattie came over and sat next to me with a sigh that stirred the air all the way to Tombstone.

"We're looking at a murderer," Mattie proclaimed after a long silence.

"He's not a murderer. It was self-defense."

"Did we kill him?" We both looked up into his folded face.

"No," I said. "Lizzy wanted us to bring him here." I turned from Pop's face to Mattie's. "She guided us all in here. And that poor damn mule. So Pop could be free of the torture of killing someone, free of the gunfighter. And get his claim back."

Mattie laughed just a little. "That mule must've really wanted him." Then the laugh stopped. "This is unbelievable. It's got to be a dream."

I smiled. "They'll be out in the hills together, at his old dead stake. Who knows, maybe that bit of rock is still alive with a little trickle of silver. They'll be there, in the wind, out there in the sage."

As I traveled over the hills with Pop and the mule, Mattie catapulted into a panic. "What are we going to tell Randall? I can't believe this. We can't just leave his body in here. We have to tell people, we have to tell someone that he died. They'll all ask why we took him in the mine." She looked at me at the height of her panic, her eyes swimming in fear. "And what the hell are we going to say?"

My heart shriveled. "I don't know."

We never had to decide.

With a shivering in the ground underneath us, the sound of the train in the tunnel rushed toward us. We looked at each other in surprise, then in fright, as the train's uninvited light grew brighter.

There was no immediate explanation, no soothing reason for us as we stood there at the dead end of the tunnel. We saw the train hit the broken track going much too fast. Sparks spewed from underneath the train's belly, and as it lurched to the place where the track ended in a scattering of rail, it thrust itself through the dirt straight for us. The train's light surrounded everything—Mattie and me, Pop, the rock, and Janice's face in the driver's seat, frozen in madness, in freedom, in fearlessness. In a brilliant instant, I was happy for Janice. Mattie had been right: Janice turned out to be profound.

She flew by us, the train screeching through the dirt as we leapt out of its way. Janice and the train crashed head first into Pop and the rock wall where he sat in his tomb. The sound became the end of the world and the lights went out as the walls broke and the ceiling began to fall in a torrent of rock and earth.

I remember the silencing around my body, the quiet rush of bones, and the big pull of lungs. Mattie's hand shoving my spine, boots slipping, spinning forward finally, running. Dirt and pieces of rock spilled onto our heads and shoulders. My arms flew as we ran, splitting the darkness between the tunnel wall and the side of the train, screaming for sky. Sky full of stars, pinched by treetops holding up a radiant white moon. I ran with blind boots, knees bouncing off the dark hard ground, hands scraping rock wall. I felt the pressure of Mattie's hand wrapped around my spine. We moved like two clumsy, ricocheting bullets, barely a foot ahead of the collapsing ceiling, pelted from behind by tumbling rock. I felt the burning effort of my chest, felt again the pull of the treetops to a sparkling sky. Demanding the sky, my body pushed against itself and lifted up. Mattie's grip left my spine, and it seemed like I was flying through the bright night stars. The treetops whispered Mattie's name as I passed over them. Where was she? The treetops said she left her hat, she'd gone back for her hat. The fire in my heart screamed into the immense sky as I flew alone, relentless, through the stars, faster, faster, reaching back for her hand, a treetop to grab, a pause for her to catch up. I heard the voices of the trees saying, *Where is she, she's gone, they'll never find each other, they'll dream always.*

I had no brakes. I tried with all my might to stop, to wait, to go back. Where was she? My hands left skin on the Copper Queen's walls as they rushed through the tunnel, pulling my blind body to safety. The echoing rumble of rock behind me pushed me faster through the black universe. I screamed Mattie's name into the jagged, rocky darkness like the shocking, soul-stopping scream of the mule.

With one sudden beam the sky came through, breaking blindness with the palest line of moonlight resting on my bloody knuckles and the glistening rock wall. The last curve of the tunnel gave into the promise of night, of star and moon and electric bulbs. Of planets and people and home.

My hand pushed into my pocket, found the key, then fumbled for the padlock. I collapsed forward on my knees with a rush of black air from my caving chest. The asphalt under my palms was warm. The taste of dry, desert night air touched my lips, my tongue, my throat. The full moon gazed at me from far away, blurring in my gritty, hot eyes. Two hands with a big turquoise ring flew up to me like a giant butterfly. They pressed my shoulders, cooling the release of lungs, of muscle. The hands gripped my arm tightly, like a tree root wrapping around itself. Mattie was there. The treetops were wrong. Her eyes dropped into mine—two dark seas, one reflecting the moon, one reflecting a mule. We sat hunched together, a creek of tears winding its way across the parking lot of the Copper Queen Mine.

High above our two breaths, and the grip of Mattie's hands, streaking through the starlit universe, a bright yellow comet passed briefly over a dusty little desert town.

Firebrand Books is an award-winning feminist and lesbian publishing house celebrating its tenth anniversary year in 1995. We are committed to producing quality work in a wide variety of genres by ethnically and racially diverse authors.

A free catalog is available on request from Firebrand Books, 141 The Commons, Ithaca, New York 14850, (607) 272-0000.